THE HAWK

Clan Ross of Skye

Hildie McQueen

USA TODAY BESTSELLING AUTHOR

The Hawk: Clan Ross of Skye
USA Today Bestselling Author
Hildie McQueen

Copyright © 2024 by Hildie McQueen
Print Edition

All rights reserved. No part of this book may be reproduced in any form or by any electronic or mechanical means—except in the case of brief quotations embodied in critical articles or reviews—without written permission.

The characters and events portrayed in this book are fictitious. Any similarity to real persons, living or dead, is purely coincidental and not intended by the author.

ISBN: 978-1-960608-06-2

Also By Hildie McQueen

Clan Ross of the Hebrides
The Lion: Darach
The Beast: Duncan
The Eagle: Stuart
The Fox: Caelan
The Stag: Artair
The Duke: Clan Ross Prequel
The Bear: Cynden

Clan Ross of Skye
The Wolf
The Hawk

Clan Ross Series
A Heartless Laird
A Hardened Warrior
A Hellish Highlander
A Flawed Scotsman
A Fearless Rebel
A Fierce Archer

Moriag Series
Beauty and the Highlander
The Lass and the Laird
Lady and the Scot
The Laird's Daughter

PROLOGUE

BEATHAN'S HAND ON her shoulder was the only warm thing she felt. The sodden clothes and cloak clung to her body seeming to add layers of cold to her already frozen limbs. Freya shivered so hard her teeth chattered.

The clouds parted allowing glimpses of the moon and star filled sky. It was as if the brightness of the heavenly planets made a mockery of what occurred that night.

They'd managed to escape on horseback heading to their uncle's home. It was pure luck that they'd heard the voices of the men looking for them.

With little to no vegetation in the area, the only cover coming from rocks or low-lying bushes, they'd had to abandon the horses. Beathan had slapped their rumps, sending the startled animals in the direction they'd been traveling, the direction that made the most sense.

Now after what seemed hours of heading toward the shoreline, they lowered to the ground, waiting to ensure no one saw them.

"We will go by sea," Beathan assured her. "It will take just a bit longer to go around to the other side of the Isle and reach Uncle Williams' lands."

Everything had gone completely and utterly wrong.

The storm they'd encountered had changed each of their

lives forever.

One for good.

The other, with deadly consequences.

CHAPTER ONE

It would take time to visit the place where he stood now and not think of the carnage that had taken place just a few months earlier.

The sounds of voices carried from inside the house out to the courtyard where Gavin Ross stood looking up at the building.

It was not his first time visiting his brother, and yet, each time he couldn't help but remember the day they overtook what had been the Mackinnon keep resulting in the late laird, their mortal enemy, slashing his own throat at realizing defeat.

In stark contrast to that day, what had been crumbling walls surrounding the keep were now sturdy and tall, and the once unkempt courtyard now housed repaired stables, pens replete with livestock, and vegetable gardens. A new guardhouse had also been built as well.

Although it was only a season since his brother, Munro, had come to live there as the new laird, many changes had occurred.

Not only to the keep but also the village and surrounding farmlands. Munro worked tirelessly to build a relationship with the local people. It was an uphill struggle for many reasons. The late laird had been a cruel and unfair man, who'd taken advantage of the people. Secondly, they were mostly

Clan Mackinnon, which meant they'd lost brothers, husbands and sons in battles against Clan Ross.

Since Munro had brought with him only a few men from Ross lands, local men, who'd plead loyalty to Munro had been hired to work as guardsmen, gardeners and stable hands. By what Gavin could tell by the surroundings, there seemed to be a good rapport between those that worked there and the Ross' who'd moved to live at the small keep.

There was a long way to go, but Gavin's brother had come a long way in building a good rapport with the community. True loyalty and trust would only come with time, there were no shortcuts when it came to building a community.

Gavin urged his horse further into the courtyard and dismounted, his boots landing solidly on the hard ground.

A young lad rushed over, his cheeks reddened by either the effort or the fact he was late in greeting a family member of his employer. "Apologies, sir. I didnae see ye arrive."

The eager expression on the boy reminded Gavin of when he'd been given his first task at his family home. Each of his brothers had begun learning the ways of keep responsibilities by working at the stables.

His father had insisted they not be treated any differently than any other workers. At the time, he'd balked considering it utterly unfair. Now he realized the wisdom of his father's ways in that he understood the responsibilities and tasks of every person that worked in a keep.

Gavin handed the young lad the horse's reins. "I only just got here. Ensure to give my steed water and oats," he instructed as the boy led his immense warhorse away. His horse, that he'd named Gregor, was an intelligent animal. Seeming to understand that he'd be fed and watered, the usually boisterous horse lowered his head in an attempt at docility and allowed the boy to lead him away.

Gavin's boots crunched solidly on the stone pathway that led to the wide arched front doorway. The front door was closed, perhaps no one had alerted his brother that someone had arrived. Either an oversight or his brother was otherwise occupied.

Gavin pushed the door open without knocking and walked into the dim cool interior.

Munro's two wolfhounds, which had been their father's, lay just outside the entrance to the great room. The dogs roused from slumber, lifting their heads to see who'd disturbed their sleep and sniffed the air. With soft barks of recognition the dogs jumped to their feet and bounded toward him, tongues lolling out of the sides of their mouths. The large beasts jumped to their hind legs, pressing paws on his chest and sides, their bodies wiggling in a dance of joy.

Unable to contain a smile, Gavin rubbed his hands down the sides of the dogs' bodies and scratched the rough fur. Since the dogs had gone to live with his brother, Gavin missed their company. Many a night one or both would find their way to his bedchamber and sleep at his feet.

"Aye, I miss ye both as well," he said as the hounds competed to claim a lick to his face.

"Brother," Munro walked toward him and the boisterous dogs. "I dinnae expect ye."

Munro was just a bit shorter than his six-foot height, with thick arms, broad chest and thick dark brown hair. A warrior through and through, Munro naturally moved with purpose, somehow managing to exude a mixture of strength and grace simultaneously.

His brother's green gaze traveled over Gavin from head to toe, inventorying him for any injuries or bruising. He understood that being second to the youngest meant his older brothers worried about his wellbeing, but at times the coddling was annoying, especially when other warriors were about. Gavin's or his younger brother Cynden's discomfort never deterred his older brothers Munro and the laird, Alexander, from doing it.

"What brings ye?" Munro made his way forward and they hugged in greeting. The feel of his brother's arms around him was familiar and comforting in a familiar sort of way.

"Must a brother have a reason to visit?" Gavin teased. "Perhaps I missed yer pretty face."

His brother's expression was serious. "I supposed all beauty is gone from the keep since my departure. All who are left are trolls."

Gavin punched him in the shoulder. "I may be a troll, but I can still beat ye in most things."

Munro was five years older than him; however, at five and thirty, his brother remained quite youthful and strongly built. Truth be told, Gavin would be hard-pressed to beat him in hand-to-hand combat.

"Perhaps in archery," Munro stated. "How are things? Did Alexander and Mother leave for Uist?" Their eldest brother and mother had traveled to visit their cousins on the Isle of Uist, which was a short distance on bìrlinn from Skye.

"Aye they did, Mother plans to return in a fortnight. Alexander will remain away longer. He wishes to learn as much as he can from Darach," he said referring to their cousin, Darach Ross, the laird of Clan Ross of Uist.

While continuing to talk of nonconsequential things, they made their way inside to the great room.

At seeing them, Munro's wife, Lila, rose from a chair next to the hearth and walked toward them. Her long skirts swayed around her legs as she moved across the room.

"How kind of ye to visit. Munro misses ye all," Lila greeted Gavin by lifting her face for him to kiss both cheeks. Since marrying his brother, the shy lass had blossomed. Although still reserved, she exuded a serene strength that wasn't evident before.

"How fare ye?" Gavin asked his brother's wife.

A soft smile on her lips, Lila slid a look to Munro then back to him, her cheeks pinkening. "I am very happy here."

It was easy to tell that both Lila and his brother were still in the throes of discovering their love for each other. The lingering looks of new lovers they exchanged were hard to ignore. He was glad for Munro, that he'd made a love match.

"I will see about something for ye to drink and eat," Lila said excusing herself.

"We will be in the study," Munro called out to Lila.

"Come, tell me all that happens," Munro said gesturing for Gavin to follow him to a room to the right of the entrance.

The room was brighter than the great room thanks to a large window that opened to the south, which meant it had sunlight all day long. It was simply furnished. Since moving in, Munro hadn't wished to keep anything that belonged to the late laird and had given away most of the furnishings and had new ones built. Aside from a table and chairs, there was a sideboard alone one walls.

While Munro held hearings from the local people in the great room, private meetings with guards and village councils were done in the study.

A housemaid entered with a large tray that held a plate of food, a pitcher and two tankards.

Despite him being family and not requiring the formality, Gavin appreciated Lila's efforts, especially at noting thinly sliced ham, his favorite, on the plate.

Munro poured ale from the pitcher into the tankards handing one to Gavin. His brother sat back in his chair and let out a long breath. "Today has been quiet. Other than a pair of farmers coming to ask about land boundaries, no one has sought a hearing."

"Do not allow yerself to trust over much," Gavin replied past the ham in his mouth. "It is too soon to expect complete peace."

Munro nodded. "I am fully aware. I ensure there is always a Ross within each group on patrols. It seems so far, they are building a camaraderie. Yet I often remind the men who came with me from Keep Ross they are not to let their guard down and to keep their eyes open."

Satisfied that his brother was being as careful as he could be, Gavin felt more at ease.

"Have ye discovered any more about the woman who washed up on shore?" Munro abruptly changed the subject to something Gavin wasn't sure he was prepared to talk about.

Gavin shook his head, immediately picturing the dark-haired woman, with almond-shaped brown eyes and a heart-shaped face. The striking beauty was shrouded in mystery, making it hard to keep curiosity at bay.

By her demeanor, always looking over her shoulder and avoiding the courtyard for extended periods, to him it was obvious they could be harboring someone in fear for their life, which meant she had enemies.

Her presence brought the possibility of danger to the clan.

Along with her brother, Freya Craig had washed up on shore after a particularly strong storm. It had been miraculous that they'd skirted the worst of the storm and had survived. Unfortunately, shortly after their small seacraft was pulled ashore and being rescued by Clan Ross guards, her brother had perished from exposure and refusing to eat or drink while at sea so that his sister could survive.

Now the woman lived at Keep Ross as a launderess, keeping her past a secret from everyone.

Gavin shook his head and blew air from his nose. "It is maddening. We have tried everything to get information about where she comes from and what caused her and her brother to flee. But she remains steadfastly silent on the subject refusing to speak of the past. For the time being, we keep her in the cottage in the courtyard. Although she works in the laundry, it is not easy for her to go from there to the main areas without being seen."

Munro's brow crinkled. "Perhaps ye and Knox can sit with her and explain it will be impossible to continue to harbor her without knowing why she escaped from wherever she came from," he said referring to their wily cousin.

"Aye, I am fully aware it must be done," Gavin said. Once again he pictured the frail beauty. Although admittedly, she was slight and seemed the type to be easily broken, he was not fooled. The woman had survived a harrowing ordeal, worked hard and steadfastly kept secrets. She was much stronger than she seemed.

"How should I begin the conversation?" Gavin was genuinely perplexed. He'd tried many different ways to ask, and each time Freya had instantly closed off, refusing to speak or even make eye contact.

Munro shrugged. "That may be a question best asked to a woman." He stood and moments later returned with Lila.

"I believe you can help Gavin out of a quandary," Munro told her motioning for her to sit.

Lowering to the chair Munro had vacated she sat perched on the edge, hands folded on her lap. "How can I help?" She gave him an inquisitive look, her face relaxed.

"I must question Freya, the woman who washed up on shore, and insist she reveal why she and her brother fled their home. Thus far she refuses to speak of it," Gavin explained. "I am nae sure how to approach her yet again and get answers."

"Ye cannae treat her as if she is a prisoner, but with kindness. Assure Freya that it is her safety ye wish to ensure."

Gavin scratched his jaw in consideration. "Nae, it is the clan's safety I wish to safeguard."

Letting out a long sigh, Lila shook her head. "What I mean is that ye should convince her that ye wish to be sure she is safe. I am sure she is already aware ye wish to keep the clan safe."

"I see," Gavin replied not quite sure he did.

"Dinnae cross yer arms when ye do." Lila's gaze went to his chest, and Gavin uncrossed his arms. "Ye must be approachable."

He exchanged looks with Munro who seemed as puzzled as him.

Gavin met Lila's gaze. "I think she is hiding from someone, either because she is avoiding an arranged marriage, or perhaps in fear of her life. Either way, we cannae continue to give harbor when she refuses to tell us why she fled her home."

"If it were me," Lila said. "If I were hiding in fear and continued to be questioned, I would in all probability flee. It could be she feels safer if the truth is hidden." She bit her bottom lip in thought. "Take her for a walk. Treat her as a friend. It could work."

"I do nae have time to coddle her. Be carefree when there is a possibility of danger…" Gavin began.

"How much danger can a scorned groom be? Or an angry father? That siblings left together points to a family matter." Lila's expression became sad in all probability remembering her own past of mistreatment.

THEY FINISHED EATING and Munro asked him to join in the guard's practice, which he did. Afterwards, the off-duty guards joined the family for last meal in the great room.

Although he missed Munro, now when they spent time together it felt more meaningful. They spend more time in conversation, and he didn't have to share the time with the other brothers or cousin. It was their private time, which Gavin treasured.

Gavin pushed back from the table and along with Munro walked out to the courtyard where the same young lad was dispatched and returned with his horse.

Once again, the brothers embraced.

"Be with care," Munro said, "Ye should nae be traveling alone. Despite us now owning the lands here, there are still those unhappy being under Clan Ross's control."

"So they would rather be ruled by a tyrant?" Gavin asked flabbergasted.

"I think it has more to do with the years of fighting against us and the death of loved ones by our swords," Munro clarified. His brother looked past the gates, his brow furrowed.

Gavin followed his line of sight waiting for his brother to continue. "I understand. For me, at times it is hard to come face to face with those I fought against, not knowing which one killed Brice."

At mentioning their dead childhood friend, Gavin's chest constricted. "Ye are a much stronger man than me. I am nae sure I could live alongside them."

"I am much stronger than ye. Ye are but a young lad still." Munro's eyes twinkled with mirth.

Once again they embraced, and Gavin mounted.

"Be with care," Munro said.

THE RIDE BACK to Keep Ross was uneventful until a wagon being driven by a bearded man came into view. The merchant brought the tarped wagon to a halt loudly greeting Gavin.

"Friend are ye headed to Tokavaig?" the man called out.

"Nae," Gavin replied. Tokavaig was a large village a short ride from Keep Ross, where he lived.

Undeterred, the man smiled widely waving for Gavin to stop. "I have many lovely wee things yer lady love would be delighted to receive. She will repay ye with great glee," the man exclaimed with a meaningful wink. "Allow me to show ye kind sir."

The sun was setting, but he was close enough to home that he'd arrive before nightfall.

Gavin neared the wagon and taking it as an agreement, the man clambered down from his seat and hurried to the back of his caravan and moments later emerged with a tray of trinkets.

Except for once, when he'd been about ten and five and infatuated with a village lass, he'd only purchased items for his mother from peddlers.

At the man lifting the tray, Gavin studied the items unsure what exactly most of them were.

"What is this?" he asked holding up a shiny bauble.

"Ah, good choice," the peddler said with a broad grin. "It can be added to a ribbon and worn as a necklace.

"A comb?" Gavin pointed at another strange pronged item.

"To comb the lush hair of yer lady love or it can be used to decorate. See the intricate detail?" the peddler explained.

They continued back and forth until finally Gavin decided to purchase the heart-shaped pendant, a wooden box, two ribbons, and a small jeweled dagger.

"Yer lady love will shower ye with kisses," the peddler happily pronounced. With surprising agility for his rather portly size the bearded man-made quick work of climbing back onto his seat and pulling the reins back to alert his horse they were to get on their way.

"Safe travels and good tidings," the peddler said with a grin as he lead the wagon to the opposite fork in the road than the way Gavin was to go.

Gavin placed the bundle of purchases in a sack that hung

from his saddle and continued to the keep. He wasn't sure who he would give the items he'd purchased to. That the lass Freya came to mind as he chose items was a bit disconcerting.

It was possible that a gift would entice her to speak. Gavin huffed. The lass was much too intelligent to be convinced with gifts. At the same time, she had nothing of her own and the items he'd purchased would be her only belongings.

He was certainly giving too much thought to the mysterious woman. It could come to be that she was married and had a husband and bairns waiting for her return. Something in his gut told him she did not belong to another, at least not willingly.

KEEP ROSS STOOD atop a hill that jutted out toward the sea. There was a drawbridge that once crossed led to the courtyard. The only other way to enter past the tall gates would be to climb up the sides of the rocky hill and breach the guarded walls.

Sheep grazed in the surrounding rugged terrain, their feet seeming sure on the craggy rocks.

Across from the keep was a tall hill upon which guard quarters had been built. It was a very fortified site upon which his ancestors had built. The only way to attack Keep Ross would be by sea and then scaling steep hillsides.

Gavin studied the sea beyond the keep, the water was calm, the waves gently lapping the shoreline.

He guided his steed across the drawbridge where guards greeted him as they turned large levers that opened the gates. Once in the courtyard, he dismounted and stretched out his stiff back. He wished for nothing more than to fall into his bed and rest.

Several warriors milled about, most had finished training for the day and were checking on their steeds before ending the day. As a warrior, the most important thing when going to battle was their weapons and their mounts. As a result, the horses were very well cared for.

Gavin led his horse to a corralled area. The stable hands were busy, so he went about removing the saddle, brushing down the horse and ensuring it had water. The animal bobbed his large head and looked around before turning away to trot to the other horses.

The small sack he'd placed the items from the peddler hung from the saddle. Gavin retrieved it and headed toward the main house. It had been a long day of travel, and although he was tired, he was in good spirits.

For a moment he considered going to Freya's cottage, but decided it was best to wait and think through how he would approach speaking to the woman as Lila had instructed. If she was truly in fear for her life, he didn't want to scare her enough to run away and end up in more danger.

BESIDES GAVIN, THE family members who lived at the keep, were his brother and laird, Alexander, his mother, his youngest brother Cynden, Cynden's wife Ainslie and his cousin Knox.

Currently Alexander and his mother were gone to visit family on the Isle of Uist.

They'd probably all retired to their rooms because no one was in the great room when he walked though, the room was all shadows and dimness without any lanterns or candles to emanate light.

To his surprise when he walked into his bedchamber, the woman who'd inhabited his thoughts stood at the foot of the bed. Freya was placing folded clothes into a trunk. She hummed quietly giving him an opportunity to study her.

Seeming to sense someone watching, she jerked up and whirled to face him, mouth forming an "O", eyes flying wide.

Her cheeks pinkened as their eyes met. "I am placing clean clothes here… sir." She stood stock still and brushed her hands down the front of the apron she wore. "If ye will excuse me." Freya took a tentative step forward but stopped at him not moving aside to let her pass.

"It is late, why are ye still working?" Gavin asked.

She pressed her lips into a tight line in thought. "I wished to finish my tasks and help Flora with hers as she fell behind. I am finished and going to the cottage now."

"I wish to speak to ye," Gavin said then looked around the room. "I suppose it would be best to do so elsewhere."

Lifting the lantern she'd probably used to find her way there, he motioned to the door, and they exited together.

Once in the corridor, he walked toward his mother's sewing room. The only woman of the family currently about was Ainslie, his brother Cynden's wife. Hopefully she wouldn't be in there at the moment.

"In here." He opened the door and waited for her to enter.

CHAPTER TWO

Freya cursed her luck at having been caught by Gavin Ross in his bedchamber. If only she'd gone earlier to deposit the clean clothes. Now he wished to speak to her. As he'd done at every opportunity, he'd question her about her past and why she'd fled her home.

Fast thuds of her heart echoed in her ears as she walked next to him. The narrow corridor made it impossible to keep her shoulder from bumping his arm on occasion despite her trying to keep as much distance as possible between them.

The whishing sounds of her heart's hammering reminded her to breath and Freya parted her lips in an attempt to catch her breath. It wasn't just the thought of the questions to come, but the fact that of all the men at Keep Ross, Gavin seemed to have a strong affect her. She could sense his presence before seeing him. A strange heat would envelope her when he was anywhere close by.

As they continued toward the sitting room, her breathing became harsher, whether from fear or something else, she wasn't sure.

Everything about the imposing man who walked beside her emanated strength and power. Although third born, there was an air of leadership about Gavin. From his towering height to the broad expanse of his shoulders, it was obvious the man was as much a warrior as he was a keen-eyed archer. The maids often spoke of his many conquests in competitions, every rendition accompanied with breathy comments on his handsome appearance.

He smelled of outdoors.

Freya dared a glance up at his profile. Admittedly, the man was gorgeous. With long-lashed green eyes under dark eyebrows, a strong jawline, and plush lips. He had light brown hair that fell in waves to his wide shoulders.

They entered Lady Ross's sitting room and not waiting for an invitation, Freya practically collapsed into the closest chair. Hoping he'd not notice the trembling of her hands she clutched them together on her lap and waited.

The only reason she'd dared to venture into his bedchamber was because the chambermaid had told her he was gone to visit his brother and would possibly not return until the following day. Now she had no recourse but to be subjected to questioning. No matter what he asked, it was not possible to say anything to him that would satisfy.

"Are ye scared of me?"

Freya's gaze flew up to his. Strange question, she considered. "I am nae." It was the truth. Yes, she found him intimidating, mainly because of his size and the fact he was a warrior.

If she was nervous, it was because of the secrets she held. Also because of how her body reacted to him, wishing to be closer, to reach and touch him.

His eyes trailed from her eyes to her mouth. Needing to catch her breath, her lips parted of their own accord they parted, her breath catching at what felt so intimate. For a moment, neither spoke nor moved, it was as if time stood still.

Freya took Gavin in. There was a shadowing of beard on his jaw that made her want to run her palm over it. His full lips were slightly parted and for a scant second, she allowed herself to imagine them against her.

Shocked at her thoughts, Freya turned to the doorway. "Is there something ye wish to speak to me about?"

He blinked as if he'd been pulled from his thoughts.

"I have something for ye." He lifted a worn leather sack and held it out.

Freya studied the item but didn't reach for it.

"Take it," he urged.

Before she could reach for it, he seemed to think better of it. Pulling it back, he shoved his hand into it retrieving a small bundle.

Flexing her fingers, Freya considered why the man would give her anything. Was it a trick?

"What is it?"

"I purchased ye a gift." He continued held it out. "Ye must accept it. I have no one else to give it to,"

It made little sense why this man would purchase her a gift. Curiosity won and Freya reached for the neatly tied bundle.

His gaze followed the progress as she grasped it. The corners of his lips lifted, and she realized he was waiting for her to open it.

With shaky fingers, she placed it on her lap, untied the string, and pulled the edges of the rough cloth apart to expose an interesting collection of items.

There was a small stone heart with a tiny loop so that it

could be used as a pendant, an intricately carved box, two ribbons, and a jeweled dagger. Of all of them, the dagger made her wonder what he was thinking.

"Why did ye get these things?" she asked noting his head titled at an angle as he studied her with interest.

His wide shoulders lifted and lowered. "I came upon a peddler when heading back from visiting my brother. The man was amicable, and we struck up a conversation. I felt as if I should purchase some items."

Unsure of what to think she frowned. "Why give them to me?"

This time only one shoulder lifted. "Ye dinnae have anything much. The peddler said women like ribbons and such." He motioned to the items on her lap.

Despite the strangeness of the situation, it was sweet of him. Freya studied the items, running her fingers over the wooden box. She adored carved boxes. Back at home, there were several on her dressing table.

Shaking off the reminder, she motioned to another item. "And the dagger?"

This time he frowned. "Every lass should keep one about her person. For protection."

Freya pulled the edges of the bundle close. "It is all very lovely. I cannae possibly accept them. Ye do nae know me, and I am sure there is another woman who would love a gift from ye."

"Do ye plan to return home and dinnae want to explain why ye have these items?" Gavin asked, his words measured.

Her breath caught as she carefully pondered how to reply. Finally Freya decided to always speak truthfully. "I will never return to where I came from."

When she didn't continue, he spoke again, "If ye worried for yer safety, I can assure ye here at Keep Ross ye are safe."

"I do feel safe here," Freya admitted.

He gave a nod. "I am glad to hear it. More than anything, my family wishes… I wish to ensure everyone within the walls of the keep are well protected. The reason I pry about ye being here is to ensure it. I must ask ye Freya. Does yer presence bring danger to my people?"

It was the question she'd been dreading. In truth, she didn't think so, but the man they'd ran from was ruthless.

Freya met his gaze. "It is doubtful anyone will ever seek me out. Yer clan is strong and powerful. I bring no threat."

If her betrothed, Tasgall Macgregor, thought she and her brother had perished at sea, then perhaps it was true. Her betrothed was a horrible person, but he didn't have any power away from Eigg. His family as also only just a family without guards or ties to the local laird.

The only thing Tasgall cared about was her family's lands and fortune. Without her, he would never be able to gain them and that was the only reason he'd search for her. If only she and Beathan had been able to reach her uncle's lands and seek shelter there. The outcome would have been so very different.

Now she had no idea what happened on Eigg. If her family had any idea that she and Beathan were gone from the Isle.

GAVIN WAS WITHIN his rights to ask whether her presence would cause strife. If she continued to refuse to give them a reason for being there, eventually Gavin's brother, the laird, would undoubtedly send her away.

"What was the reason ye and yer brother fled yer homeland?" Gavin asked another difficult question.

Turning the words over in her mind, Freya wondered how much she could reveal. She'd been unable to ascertain if Clan Ross was allied with anyone on Eigg.

"We had to leave. It was imperative. We were in danger there," she finally offered.

He studied her for a long moment, making it impossible for her to look away.

"How would ye react in this situation if I was to show up at yer home refusing to give any information?" he asked, not breaking eye contact.

Freya thought about it. "I am nae sure to have been as generous as yer family were to my brother and me. There is nae reason to trust me, but I give ye my word that I will leave if at any moment my presence can cause turmoil. Though let me assure you again that I am quite certain no one will ever come looking for me."

By the long exhalation and lips pressed into a tight line, he wasn't satisfied with her replies. There was little Freya could do. To divulge who she was and where she was from could mean she'd be taken back to a place where her future was not guaranteed.

"My brother will return in a pair of months. At that time, he will decide whether ye can remain or not. Ye should prepare yerself for where ye will go if he decides ye cannae remain." He stood and she followed suit.

Freya held up the bundle. "Please take this."

His hand covered hers and a chill traveled up her arm, it was all Freya could do not to close her eyes and relish the feel of his touch. Instead she waited for him to take the bundle. Instead he wrapped his large hand around hers, tightening her hold on the bundle.

"I bought it for only ye. Would ye insult me by refusing my gift?" When she lifted her gaze he turned and walked away.

For a moment, Freya watched his retreating back, her mind awhirl. Clutching the bundle against her chest, she let out a long breath. Catching herself, Freya chided. He'd only done it to be kind, not because he felt any kind of attraction.

Possibly he'd done it to build trust between them, so that she'd divulge more information. Best not to allow her overly romantic mind to make more than there was of the situation.

Despite everything, Freya's lips curved as she held the small bundle up to her nose and sniffed. The wrapping smelled of outdoors, just like he had.

Here she was fantasizing, and Gavin was in all probability frustrated at her for being less than forthcoming with information. Freya didn't blame him. In his place, she would feel the same.

Perhaps it would be best for her to make inquiries to the staff and find out as much as she could about Clan Ross' relationships with clan Macgregor. If there was even the slightest threat of harm from them, she could explain everything to Gavin.

She tucked the bundle of items under her arm and hurried from the sitting room, down the stairs, and outside. Once there, she crossed the courtyard and went to one of a row of tiny one room cottages.

There were servant rooms in the proper house; however, she'd not been asked to move there. After a conversation with the main housekeeper, Freya gathered it was because they didn't wish a stranger inside the main house where the family lived. She was not trusted, which was both sad and understandable.

As she crossed the courtyard, Freya bent her head blinking back tears of frustration and sorrow. For the first time in her life, she was utterly alone. Never in her life had she felt such despair and hollowness.

On the Isle of Skye, she had absolutely no one to call a friend or family. The only person she could trust was herself, and it was proving to be so very difficult to make it from one day to the next without falling apart while relying on her strength alone.

As she closed the door behind and latched it, tears spilled down her cheeks at the physical ache in her chest.

How lonely she was.

THE REPETITION OF the same activities each day was soothing in a way. Freya started every morning with breakfast in the kitchens with other servants and then went directly to the laundry where she accomplished the same tasks.

The work was strenuous but simple enough. It consisted of large pots of boiling water and lye being stirred by women with large wooden paddles. Lads constantly hurried in with buckets of water or logs for the large fire in the hearth.

Freya, along with another young woman, rinsed the clothes in tubs, inspected them for stains or tears, and then hung them up to dry outside.

By the afternoon, the room was oppressively hot, but Freya barely noticed, her mind on the conversation with Gavin the day before.

She'd slept fretfully. The entire night she wondered if she'd disclosed enough that the family would allow her to remain and be safe, or not enough and she'd be told to leave when the laird returned.

Once in the cabin the night before, she'd once again opened the bundle and examined the items Gavin had given her closely. Each one was specific and quite pretty. She wanted to believe he'd chosen each one thinking of her, but common sense interfered making her realize the peddler had probably suggested what he purchase. In the middle of the night, she'd gotten up, wrapped a shawl around her shoulders and went outside to look up at the sky.

She lifted a tunic from the water and inspected it for tears just as Una, the head mistress, appeared in the doorway. The older woman came to stand near her and spoke in a low tone so no one else could hear.

"I saw ye leave yer cottage quite late last evening. Ye seemed quite forlorn. Is there something wrong?"

Freya considered that there was little privacy in a keep. She decided to reply honestly. "I have moments when I miss my family terribly," Freya replied truthfully. "It aches here in my chest." She pressed her flattened palm between her breasts.

"It is understandable," the woman said patting her shoulder. "Once the clothing is hung to dry, everyone can stop for the day and rest," she called out. "It is much too hot in here."

"Thank ye," one of the laundresses piped up and Una continued, "There will be visitors tomorrow, which means ye will be helping the kitchen staff and the chambermaids. Ensure to rest as much as ye can."

It wasn't long before Freya entered the staff kitchens with the rest of the laundry workers. The women discussed their day, the men they were interested in, and other gossip. Freya waited for the opportune time to ask about the visitors.

"What other clans usually visit here?"

The others mulled her questions and several replied.

"Clan MacLachlan."

"Clan MacLeod."

"Landowners from neighboring areas."

Another one piped up. "'Tis the laird from Barra, The MacNeil, who travels through here tomorrow."

At the name of the visitors being divulged Freya relaxed, letting out a long breath of relief. Thankfully, she didn't know anyone from there.

"What are we to do differently tomorrow?" she asked, not really caring what the reply was, but wanting to have a reason for the first question.

"Mostly ye will be in here to help the kitchen staff," Una told her. "It depends on how large the party is traveling with the laird, but three of ye from the laundry will help with the cleaning and freshening of the bedchambers."

Once meal was over, everyone dispersed eager to be with family or get on with whatever was planned for the rest of the day.

Freya lingered in the kitchens helping with washing up. She wasn't eager to return to her empty cottage.

IT WAS GOOD to have work to keep her busy during the day,

but the evenings seemed to stretch forever. The silence was unbearable, making Freya miss the noisiness of the interior of the house.

Her home back on Eigg had been much like the Ross keep. Her father was a wealthy merchant, who'd purchased lands when quite young and built a beautiful house for his bride. Together they'd raised Freya and her brother, Beathan in a home where they constantly entertained visitors from different lands and from the surrounding areas. Hers had been a warm and welcoming home.

Most of the time they'd gotten along well with the neighboring landowners, and her father did his best to be on good terms with the local laird. It wasn't until just a year earlier that everything had gone horribly wrong.

The sound of voices outside shook her from memories of the past that would only serve to make her spend the night crying. Freya grabbed her shawl from a hook by the door and went out to the courtyard.

She scanned the courtyard hoping to see women about with whom to talk with to pass the time. Near the well, two women stood chatting. One was a chambermaid called Flora. The other a woman called Senga, who lived in the village but seemed to visit the keep often with her father.

"Freya, thank ye for helping me yesterday with the bedchambers," Flora said in greeting when she neared. "I would have nae finished my duties otherwise."

"I am glad to keep busy," she replied.

"It seemed all the Ross men needed clean tunics at the same time," Flora exclaimed with a dramatic roll of her eyes. "I dinnae mind, except that Una wished for us to change all the linens on the beds as well."

"I would nae mind washing Gavin Ross' tunics," Senga said, her eyes moving toward the house. "Is he about today?"

Flora shrugged and Freya remained silent. Although she'd seen him earlier, she wouldn't know if he was about since she spent most of her days in the servant's quarters, which were away from the main rooms of the house.

As if summoned, Gavin and his cousin, Knox, walked from the training field into the courtyard. Deep in conversation, the handsome duo didn't notice them.

"Oh my," Senga said, pushing errant hair away from her face. "There he is now."

Freya wished she could hide, but there was nowhere to duck behind. The last thing she wished for is for either of the men to be reminded of her existence and perhaps ask to speak to her again.

Unfortunately, they walked toward where they stood. In all probability to seek a drink of water from the well.

Senga took a dramatic deep breath as the men neared. "Mister Gavin, how are ye today?"

Both Flora and Freya took a step away from Senga. Freya took it a step back further and moved to stand behind Flora, wishing against hope not to be noticed.

"I am well, Senga," Gavin replied. "Ye came with yer father?"

"Aye, he is with Alpin," she said referring to the man in charge of the storehouse.

There was silence and Freya held her breath. Too curious to see what happened, she peered from behind Flora.

Both Ross men were looking toward the storehouse from

where an older man had emerged and walked toward them.

It was the best time to walk away and hopefully not be noticed. Just as she took a step away, Flora spoke up. "Do ye wish to walk with me to gather flowers for the great room?"

Both Knox and Gavin turned to Flora, who blushed brightly at the attention. Gavin's flat gaze slid to Freya for a moment. "Where are ye going to pick flowers, Flora?"

The poor girl was flustered and without speaking pointed to the gates. Senga glared at Flora for taking the attention away from her.

"Th-the field just there," Flora stuttered and tugged Freya's hand. "Come let us hurry before it becomes dark."

Gavin held a hand up blocking their progress. "I will walk with ye to the gates and ensure a guard keeps watch over ye. Although it has been peaceful, we cannae be too careful."

Both Flora and Freya exchanged confused looks. They'd gone to and from the keep many times and never been escorted.

Senga looked longingly to Gavin hoping to be invited along. Unfortunately, her father had neared and began a discussion with Knox, which meant she had to remain behind.

"I will fetch a basket from the garden shed," Flora said and hurried away leaving Freya standing alone with Gavin. Her stomach sank when he studied her for a moment.

"I-I must return the items ye gave me…I cannae accept…" Freya began.

"The items are yers to do with whatever ye wish. I donnae expect anything in return."

Once again they fell silent. Gavin reached up and rubbed the nape of his neck. "There are visitors tomorrow and without my brother here, I must greet them and stand in my brother's stead."

It was a strange thing that he mentioned it to her, but by his expression, Freya could see it worried him. Her brother had often been anxious if ever their father was away, and he would have to host visitors.

"It is always safe to speak of sport and to invite them for a hunt. My father said the more he hunted or fished with a visitor the less time they had to sit about and talk," Freya offered.

Gavin's lips curved into a smile that reached his eyes making it hard to look away.

"I will do just that. The weather is perfect for hunting," he said.

Flora neared with two baskets and handed one to Freya just as Gavin called a guard to come to them.

The man looked them over with disinterest, obviously as confused as they'd been at the request to be looked after. He turned his attention back to Gavin.

"Ensure to keep watch. They are to remain in the field, not venture into the woods."

The man nodded as they began walking toward the gate. Much to her consternation, Gavin remained alongside.

"What else does yer father do for visitors?"

"Are ye nae here when visitors come?" Freya asked, confused.

"I avoid it."

She considered her answer. "Mother and Father would hire local musicians to entertain during the meal. They would also invite neighbors to attend last meal, so that the visitors would have others to speak to."

"Do they entertain often?" he asked, brow furrowed.

"They did."

"Ye have been very helpful," he said, giving her a long look before walking away.

"It is strange that he asks ye those questions," Flora said watching Gavin walk away. "I wish he would have asked me what my parents do when visitors come."

"What do they do?" Freya asked studying her new friend.

"Mother cooks and Father complains," Flora said with a giggle.

Freya smiled. "I supposed my parents did the same."

Looking over her shoulder to the retreating Gavin, Freya wondered if he really wished to know how to entertain guests or if he was hoping to get more information about her past. She went over what she'd said as they picked flowers deciding she'd not divulged anything pertinent.

At least she hoped she'd not.

CHAPTER THREE

"Did ye find out anything more?" Knox asked when Gavin caught up with him entering the house.

He nodded, sliding a glance toward the gates. The women would be nearing the field now and would begin picking flowers. He wondered if it meant Freya would come into the house to help set up the flowers. He cleared his throat. What did it matter?

"Aye, I did. It is obvious she comes from an affluent family. When I mentioned having visitors and not knowing how to entertain them, she gave me some insight." Gavin repeated what Freya had said about her father.

"That is interesting," Knox said. "What else?"

"She referred to her parents in the past tense. I am nae sure if it is because she spoke of the past, or because they are no longer alive."

They walked into the great room where his youngest brother, Cynden, and his wife sat. Ainslie wrung her hands and looked to Gavin. "I wish yer mother was here. I have never entertained alone. I am nae sure what to do."

A thought occurred. "Ye can ask the woman Freya to help ye. She seemed well versed in the entertainment of visitors." Gavin looked to Cynden. "I just had an interesting conversation with the lass."

"If she can help, that would be wonderful." Ainslie looked to her husband. "Can ye have someone fetch her?"

"She is currently in the field picking flowers for the tables with Flora," Gavin mentioned, earning a quizzical look from Cynden.

He shrugged. "I have to act interested in what she does to find out who exactly she is."

Knox's brows rose and the corner of his lips curved. "I am sure the fact she's a bonnie lass makes it oh so difficult for ye."

Letting out a huff, Gavin motioned a young guard over. "Go to the field and tell Flora that both she and Freya need to come and see Lady Ainslie after picking flowers."

"Tell them to bring the flowers and green branches as well," Ainslie added. With a grateful look at Gavin, she whirled and hurried away.

"My wife will nae sleep tonight," Cynden explained and shook his head. "I dinnae understand why she is so nervous."

The cook entered and walked toward them. "Of course, the mistress is fraught. There is much to do. Any shortcomings with the meal or the house will be attributed to her lack of hosting abilities."

With pursed lips, she glanced around the great room then gave both Gavin and Knox a pointed look. "Do ye wish for a late repast since the pair of ye were nae at last meal?"

Gavin's stomach replied with a rumble. "Aye."

He and his cousin sat at the table closest to the kitchens along with Cynden and discussed the following day while eating. Not long later, the leader of the wall guards joined them wishing to be informed what to expect.

Just as they finished their meal, Freya and Flora appeared

and waited at the entrance.

Ainslie hurried to them, and the trio went to another table where small baskets and vases of all sizes had been set up. Together they began putting the flowers and branches into them, the entire time discussing where they would be placed. As far as Gavin could tell, Ainslie had yet to ask Freya about the next day.

"Ainslie has met the MacNeil's daughters before," Cynden said. "It does nae stop her from being nervous. Do we know what his plans are?"

"He is good friends with Darach," Knox said, referring to their influential cousin in Uist.

"Although the MacNeil travels through, Alex wishes for us to ensure we offer the best hospitality and invite him to remain for a pair of days," Gavin explained. "They are on their way to visit Clan MacLachlan, his wife's family."

"This is a purely social visit, however, it is always beneficial to form ties with other clans. The MacNeil's of Barra are a good ally to have," Knox stated.

"Understood," Cynden said. "I will speak to the men and plan a friendly competition with his guards."

The women continued to decorate, each placing the vases and baskets on surfaces around the room. Gavin noticed that the servant girl, Flora went up the stairs with two vases, which he assumed would be placed in the guest bedchambers.

Freya remained in the room, making quick work of placing flowers on tables and side tables, sometimes swapping them out if not satisfied.

"She is well versed in preparing for visitors," Knox said under his breath. "Whoever she is, it is obvious the lass is highborn."

"I think the same," Gavin replied.

When Ainslie went to Freya, he strained to hear the conversation. "I hear ye may be able to help me with hosting. I am so very nervous."

"Ye should nae be. Mother always said to speak of something ye are familiar with, such as gardening, cooking, sewing and such and ask about the guests' interests. Mother insisted it is better to have companionable silence than continuous babble."

Ainslie gave a nervous giggle. "I will try to remember that." Seeming to further consider, Ainslie asked. "What was yer role when visitors came?"

Thankfully Freya didn't seem to notice that Ainslie sought to gather information.

"I did whatever Mother did. Sat with the guests, kept the conversation going. Accompanied them for walks about the garden and went with guests on excursions to the nearby village."

Ainslie slid a look toward where he sat when Freya was not looking, and he made a circling motion with his hand for her to keep asking questions.

"Ye are obviously better suited for this than I will ever be," Ainslie said. "Mother and Father dinnae entertain much. Most of our visitors were family."

"We had family visit as well," Freya said with a soft smile.

"I miss my home," Ainslie said with a forlorn sigh. "But I will never regret life with Cynden."

Gavin wanted to roll his eyes. Why had Ainslie strayed from questioning Freya.

"I can imagine," Freya replied, her expression neutral. It could be, she didn't miss anyone by her lack of expression.

"Aye, well, I would say this looks quite nice. Will ye please remain nearby tomorrow. I may have to seek ye out," Ainslie said looking at the surfaces they'd decorated.

Freya nodded. "Of course."

"Perhaps one day I can visit yer home." Ainslie said and quickly added. "I'm sorry, I know ye prefer not to speak of yer past."

Freya whispered something Gavin couldn't hear, then she moved away from Ainslie to picked up stray cuttings and walked from the great room.

Moments later Ainslie neared and gave him a sad look. "Her parents are both dead, no one she lived with remains."

"How do ye know this?" Gavin asked.

Ainslie shook her head and let out a breath. "She said there was no one left at her home to return to."

THE LAIRD, ALONG with his wife, his son, and accompanying guards arrived the next day. Any trepidations about the visit were dispersed as the man's demeanor was quite pleasant. The son was about five and twenty and had apparently had previously met a few of the Ross guards who'd come to Skye from Uist. The son and guards ate together and went about their day with plans for a friendly archery competition.

The conversations between the MacNeil's and his family flowed easily, and Gavin was glad for it.

As they ate, Laird MacNeil spoke to Gavin. "There is only

one wife about. Do ye and Alexander nae plan to marry soon?"

It seemed a strange question coming from a man. Perhaps he was just making conversation. "Our brother Munro, who is second born is also married. He lives at a separate keep."

When the man remained silent, Gavin continued. "I would like to marry and have bairns someday." Gavin couldn't help but scan the room searching for Freya. That it was his initial reaction was troublesome.

The laird nodded. "It is part of life. To find a good woman to share one's life with." He directed a smile to where his wife sat with Ainslie.

"Do ye enjoy hunting?" Gavin asked, not wishing to continue the conversation on marriage. If the man had been asked by family to find a husband for some single lass in Barra, he didn't plan to be the one chosen.

The older man's eyes twinkled with mirth, having obviously suspected the diversion in conversation. "I do indeed."

Cynden leaned forward to meet the visiting laird's eyes. "Our lead guard has set up a small competition for everyone tomorrow in the nearby forest."

"THEY WERE MOST delightful," Ainslie exclaimed as they watched the MacNeil and his family take their leave early in the morning, two days later. "His wife is very excited about visiting her family."

Cynden pulled his wife to his side and pressed a kiss to her temple. "Ye were a perfect hostess."

"I would nae have been able to do it without Freya's help.

She remained near so I could ask questions. She is a godsend."

As they walked inside, Gavin pulled Ainslie aside. "Did you find out anything else about Freya's past in these last couple days?"

Ainslie gave him an apprehensive look. "She is a lovely woman who misses her life and her family. I believe she is here because she had no other choice but to leave her home behind. I wish there was something more we could do for her. She is so very sad."

When Gavin gave her a questioning look, Ainslie sighed.

"Very well, this is what I gathered. She is from an isle. She only had the one brother. Her mother loved growing flowers and her father was a kind and well-liked man. And as I told ye, both parents are dead. I wonder if there is more family, but I didn't want to press her for anymore."

"Is that all."

Ainslie huffed. "It is doubtful our clan has anything to worry about. Let her be." The spirited lass walked away from him signaling the conversation was over.

STANDING IN FOR Alexander was exhausting. Gavin spent half of the day listening to grievances from villagers and farmers, several times, having to break apart brawling men. Most of the arguments were easily solved once he asked questions clarifying each side's point of view and considered both sides.

It was past time for the midday meal when he turned to Cynden, who looked as tired as he felt. "I dinnae know how Alex does this every day," Gavin complained, as he stood and stretched. "I am tired and hungry."

Only a few people remained but seemed content to wait

since a meal would be served soon.

Wishing for a moment alone, he headed to the stairs only to stop when a guard tapped him on the shoulder. "A distraught woman with bairns and her parents are outside asking to speak to ye."

He glanced toward the interior, but Cynden was gone. He'd walked away as soon as Gavin had stood.

"Why did she nae come inside?" Gavin asked.

The guard shook his head. "I dinnae know. She is quite hysterical."

Together, they walked out to the courtyard to find the sobbing woman flanked by an older couple. Behind them in the back of the cart were four children of varying ages, some of them were also crying.

At seeing him the woman crumpled and began wailing, having to be held up by her companions.

"My Edgar. My Edgar," she said between sobs. "He is dead!"

"What happens?" Gavin asked the older man who'd accompanied her, as it seemed doubtful that the crying woman could speak clearly.

"He is dead, her husband is dead," the older man said in a shaky voice. "Someone killed him." He shook a fist. "And we know who."

"Ye must punish the man who killed my Edgar," the crying woman screamed. "The bastard killed a kind man. The father of my bairns."

At the words, the children began crying harder. Thankfully Una appeared and motioned another servant girl over. Together they helped the children climb down from the back of the wagon and guided them to the kitchens.

Obviously having overheard the commotion, Cynden hurried out to join him.

Together they managed to convince the woman and her companions to come into the keep to the great room. Once there, the woman was given honeyed mead to help calm her. She was a pitiful sight. Red swollen eyes. Hair and clothing askew.

"Explain what happened," Gavin asked in a soft tone. He'd hoped something like this would not occur in Alexander's absence. But here they were, someone had been killed and he prayed to God the killer would be easy to find.

After drinking the mead, the woman calmed and mopped her face with the corner of her shawl.

The elderly man was obviously the spokesman. "Her husband, Edgar, was returning from the village. We live just outside of Tokavaig, ye see. We raise chickens, sell the birds and eggs." He took a breath. "I hear he argued with one of yer guards. It has to be Hendry who attacked and killed him."

At the mention of the name, Cynden and Gavin exchanged alarmed looks. Hendry was one of their guards, an able warrior and friend to them both. Although very much a warrior, it was hard to believe Hendry would commit murder.

"Why do ye accuse one of my men?" Gavin asked.

"They argued at the tavern. Everyone saw it. I was told Edgar hit yer guard with a tankard. He was seen leaving the tavern after Edgar."

Gavin listened and waited for the man to be silent. "I promise that we will find out exactly what occurred."

"Bring him here, I want to hear him admit what he did,"

the widow demanded, suddenly finding the strength to speak clearly. "He must be punished."

"Ye mourn. If I were in yer place, I too would be demanding justice. First, I will go to yer home with ye. I wish to see the injuries. Once that is done, I will speak to those who claim to have witnessed all that occurred. The person responsible for Edgar's death will be punished. Ye have my word."

"Bring him here now! I want to look into his eyes!" The grieving woman screamed and collapsed against the older woman. "He must admit it," she murmured seeming to run out of energy.

He motioned a pair of guards over. "Where is Hendry?"

One replied. "On patrol on the northern shore, with three others."

Gavin already knew, but asked so that the grieving family would hear. "Go fetch him. Do nae speak to him of this. Confine him to his quarters until I can speak with him." The men gave both him and the grieving family questioning looks and then hurried away to do as told.

After more conversation back and forth, the trio finally seemed convinced Gavin would see to finding the truth.

"We will go with ye to yer home and see for ourselves what happened," Gavin informed them.

He left Cynden to see after things in the keep, and then he and Knox rode out with the anguished family.

"They blame Hendry?" Knox stated, incredulous. "Of all the warriors, Hendry is the most levelheaded."

"Aye," Gavin replied. "I find it strange to hear that he argued at the tavern. Drunkenness brings out the worst in a man, but I still cannae believe it. Hendry is nae one to drink over much."

The people in the wagon were a sad lot. Fortunately, they would be able to continue to support themselves with the chickens. And yet, losing a husband and father was not something that would be easy to overcome.

Knox studied him, his cousin's dark gaze taking him in. "It is nae Hendry."

"What if it is?" Gavin asked and let out a breath. "I am nae prepared to punish a friend."

Jaw set, Knox shook his head. "It is nae Hendry," he repeated.

CHAPTER FOUR

It took a pair of hours to arrive at the humble but well-kept house. Despite the lack of any outward signs, a deep sadness seemed to hover over the area. Such was sorrow, Gavin mused. It was not just something seen, but a tangible almost touchable thing.

One by one, assisting one another, the grief-stricken family climbed from the wagon. Carrying a bairn on her shoulder, the older woman ushered the other three children toward the house. The widow, helped by the older man, hesitated at the doorway, in all probability not wishing to see her husband's body. Not wanting to face the harsh reality she'd been thrust into.

Once she entered, her wails emanated from the interior.

There was nothing that could be done to alleviate the woman's sadness, as she mourned for her husband. Neither words nor gestures meant anything to someone mad with grief.

The older man remained outside, he looked toward the house; his face etched with sadness. "He was my daughter's husband. A good hardworking man. Didnae deserve to be killed. Never did harm to anyone. The worse he did was to have an ale too many at the tavern some days before returning home."

The house was a short ride from the village, the road to and from was well traversed, it was entirely possible others could have ridden past Edgar on his way from the tavern. There could have been witnesses.

Gavin realized that he and Knox had a long day ahead. They would leave no stone unturned. Someone had to have seen or heard something. If it meant stopping every person they saw and going to each surrounding house and farm, he would do it.

Studying the surroundings, he could see the road and to the rear of house to open fields where a herd of sheep grazed.

"Whose lands are those?" he asked the man.

"They are Clan Ross lands to the hills there," the man replied pointing. "Past that are Mackinnon lands."

Knox frowned. "They belong to Munro now, do they not?"

"Aye, they are now my brother's lands. He has made every effort to speak to everyone who lives on the lands. I am certain he knows who lives near."

"Tell us what you think happened," Knox said to the older man. Now that there was a bit of calm, the wails had subsided, it was possible the man knew things he'd not divulged in front of his daughter.

The old man seemed to deflate at having to recount the sad story. "I like to go for short walks to be sure the chickens haven't wandered too far. Most days, I see Edgar arriving back from the village. I help him unload any unsold birds and see about sweeping out the wagon so he can go inside and spend time with the family.

He was nae back. It seemed strange as it was late, even if he would have stopped at the tavern. He always goes…er went very early, at dawn and it is his habit to return from the market before last meal. When I walked to the edge of the road there." He pointed to the area.

The older man closed his eyes and grimaced, as if the memory of what had occurred was physically painful.

"I saw the wagon on the side of the road, there by the gathering of trees. By the way it was lopsided, and Edgar was nae calling out, I knew something was wrong. So I rushed to see about Edgar. I thought he may have drunk overly much."

He paused and cleared his throat, seeming to compose himself. "It was then I saw all the blood and realized he had been injured. He'd not been there earlier, so I imagine the horse must have continued forward until almost home."

The man wiped both hands down his face. "I was nae sure what to do. It was obvious he was dead. I brought him to the house. The oldest boy, my wife, and my daughter helped me get him down. I left then and rode to the village tavern, he would sometimes go there ye see," the older man said.

Gavin and Knox remained silent, allowing the man to continue without interruption.

His sad gaze moved toward the village. "It was there I was told what happened earlier at the tavern."

It was as if speaking took all his strength, the man sagged further, his thin shoulders rounded. "Nothing else makes any sense. The money he made from selling birds remained in his purse. He was nae robbed."

"I wish to see the wounds," Gavin stated.

The older man motioned to the doorway. "Very well."

The interior of the house was surprisingly well lit, the curtains pulled away from the windows to allow for sunlight.

Atop a side table a lantern gave that side of the kitchen an eerie glow.

The dead man's wife sat in a chair, her hand upon the table upon which her husband's body was laid. Her children and the older woman were gathered around her, all of them were silent in that moment.

"I must see the injury," Gavin explained. The widow gave a barely perceptive nod, and the older woman ushered the children to another room.

After a moment, the older man took his daughter by the shoulders, turning her to face him. "Come my sweet. Allow yerself a moment of rest."

Silently, the grieving woman allowed her father to guide her away.

Gavin pushed up the dead man's torn tunic and exposed a jagged cut across his chest and a deep puncture under his ribs on the left side of his body. Edgar had been cut across and then speared straight through with a sharp sword. From the cuts on his hands, it was obvious that the poor man had tried to defend himself. Without a weapon, he would have had little chance of surviving.

Knox shook his head, jaw tight. "Whoever did this, had no mercy."

There was a soft cry followed by a thud as the widow fainted. For a short time she would be in peace. Gavin neared and lifted her from the floor to gently place her on a cot.

The older man lingered near the doorway. He looked to the dead man and then to Gavin. "We must have justice."

"Ye have my word. We will find out what happened to him," Gavin replied. Fury enveloped him. He'd never understood how anyone could attack a defenseless person. Whoever killed this man was without honor.

Whoever attacked the defenseless man was a coward.

In silence, Gavin and Knox mounted and rode from the dead man's house toward the village. It was a well-traveled road with little in the way of foliage blocking views to the front and back. To their right there were groupings of trees every so often, but for the most part it was a view of sloping valleys and hills. To their right every so often herds of sheep or a scattering of cows were visible.

"What do ye think?" Knox asked.

"I cannae think of why anyone would attack an unarmed man who seemed to not be doing more than riding home. Perhaps he happened upon something, or someone, he should nae have."

Gavin scanned the surroundings. Other than someone hiding in woods on one side of the road, there was no reason to expect anything nefarious to occur in that particular area.

There were just two plots of land with homes along the opposite side of the road from the forest that led to the village.

When riding up to the first house, they neared and were greeted by a woman who waved them closer. She walked from inside a pig pen with an empty bucket in her hands. The unmistakable odor of pigs carried with her.

At them dismounting, she looked on with a worried expression. "I apologize sirs, I didnae expect my laird's family to visit," she said. "All I can offer ye is cold water from the well."

"That would be perfect, I am parched," Knox said with a smile. Immediately the woman beamed at his enthusiasm.

"Which way madam?" Knox asked exuding his well-practiced charm, while motioning for the woman to walk first then fell into step alongside."

As they made their way to her front door, Gavin walked past to the well, dropped the bucket, and drew it up. Water was poured into two chipped cups the woman had rushed from inside with. They drank the cool refreshment.

"Did ye see Edgar, the chicken farmer ride by earlier today?" Knox asked the woman who looked back and forth between them.

"Aye, I believe I did. He travels past frequently, to and from the village."

"Was he going or returning from the village when ye saw him?" Gavin asked.

The woman pondered and then shook her head. "It was early, so he was headed there. I didnae see him after."

"What of other riders?" Gavin asked. "Anyone that took yer interest?"

After a short moment, the woman shook her head. "Nay, not even a peddler today."

They thanked the woman after establishing that she'd not seen either Edgar or Hendry later that day.

The next house was a bit larger than the woman's. They were greeted by a stout bearded man who stood with both arms crossed over his chest with a dagger fisted in his right hand. It wasn't a particularly welcoming stance, which made Gavin consider whether the man had ever come to the keep and met the laird's family.

"What do ye want?" The man's eyes narrowed not showing any fear, which was admirable.

They remained mounted. "We are here to ask ye about Edgar," Knox said staring down at the man.

The man's eyes narrowed. "What about him?"

When both of them dismounted, the man looked them up and down. "Are ye the laird's men?"

Hungry and tired, Gavin wasn't in the mood to explain himself, he nodded. "Aye, we are. Edgar from up the road. Do ye know him?"

The man's stance relaxed somewhat. "Aye, what of it?"

Knox spoke next. "He was killed earlier today. Did ye seem him travel past here today?"

The man's eyes widened, and he lowered his arms. "He's dead? What happened?"

"Stabbed," Knox stated.

"Did ye see him?" Gavin repeated.

The man looked in the direction of Edgar's house and nodded. "I saw him ride past toward where he lives. Seemed still alive to me. I was a ways back away from the road, but I can see well enough."

"Did anyone else ride past just before or after?"

The man scratched his beard. "Just before seeing Edgar, I saw a group of men, perhaps six, on horseback. They were nae on the road; they were over there along the trees." He pointed to the trees.

"I didnae see anyone else today when I was out."

Gavin and Knox exchanged looks. "What direction were the group of men headed then?" Knox asked.

"They lingered on the edge of the woods for a bit, then they were gone."

Gavin had a bad feeling about the group of men. "Did ye

recognize any of them?"

The man shook his head. "Too far to see their faces clearly."

They spoke to the man for a bit longer. After learning of Edgar's death, he dropped the tough façade and assured he'd go and check on the family. Other than seeing the men along the forest, he didn't have any other information that was helpful.

After mounting once again, a weariness took over Gavin. It wasn't going to be a simple matter to figure out what had occurred to Edgar. No matter how tired, he was responsible for Edgar's family, the guard Hendry and anyone else who could be in danger.

They rode to the edge of the tree line and peered through the trees. A cold wind blew rustling the leaves, feeble rays of the sun filtered through the thick foliage, giving the area an eerie appearance.

"We should go to the tavern and then back to the keep," Gavin said, not looking away from the trees. If there were six or more men hiding there, it would be foolish for just two of them to ride into unknown danger.

No matter what the last man they'd spoken to thought to have seen, didn't mean he counted the correct number. And even if there were men lurking among the trees, it could be they did not kill Edgar.

There was the fact of the argument between Edgar and Hendry. Too much drink brought consequences and sometimes men acted out of character. It was best to go to the tavern and ask questions. After they'd return to Keep Ross and speak to Hendry.

"If the men he saw at the forest were from beyond, it could be that some of the Mackinnon warriors who fled have returned," Knox said.

"I am thinking the same," Gavin replied as they guided their steeds toward the village. "But we must ask questions and find out what occurred at the tavern. It is best to have as much information as possible before speaking to Hendry."

ONCE ENTERING THE village, they went directly to the tavern. Despite the late hour, there were only a pair of men sitting at tables, one was slumped over, snoring loudly. The stale air smelled of ale and cooked fish, not exactly an enticing combination.

"How is it my humble tavern is graced by Ross men?" The tavern keep, a burly man with a thick beard, called Angus, yelled out when they entered.

Two tankards of ale were placed on the surface of the long counter the man stood behind.

Angus was a menacing looking man with beefy arms and thick shoulders, it was rare that anyone pushed their luck against him.

"Were ye here when Edgar came in yesterday?" Gavin asked.

The man gave them a quizzical look. "Aye, I was."

"Did anything of note happen while he was here?" Knox asked next.

Angus shrugged. "He and one of yer guards, Hendry, argued."

Not surprising the man was not going to divulge more information than needed. Especially when the men at one of the tables sat up straighter and watched the interaction.

Gavin gave Angus a pointed look. "What exactly happened?"

Once again the barkeep shrugged. "Nothing more than a drunk man losing his temper. Edgar hit Hendry with his tankard and Hendry shoved him away. That seemed the end of it to me."

"Did either make threats to the other?" Knox asked.

The barkeep gave a noncommittal grunt and shook his head.

This was becoming a chore. Gavin drank the ale down. "When Edgar left, was he alone?"

At this point, it was becoming clear Angus was annoyed. "I have nothing more to say. What is this all about anyway?"

Knox and Gavin exchanged looks. Finally Knox leaned closer to Angus. "Edgar was killed on his way home. Were ye annoyed at him and followed him out perhaps?"

The bearded man's eyes grew wide. "Ed-Edgar left alone. I remained here, 'ave remained since. Ye can ask anyone."

The barkeep inhaled loudly. "That I can recall Hendry left much later." He looked around the tavern and motioned to the two men at the nearby tables. "Neither of them were here then. I didnae see anyone follow Edgar out."

The man blew out a breath. "Poor man."

After placing a pair of coins on the table's surface, they left with no more information than when they'd arrived. It was disheartening that it was still possible that the guard had killed Edgar, but the road to the keep was in a different direction than Edgar's house. There was no way to establish which direction Hendry had gone. The people they'd questioned earlier had not seen him.

"By the time we get to the keep, there would be little light. Any more travel will have to wait until tomorrow. For now, let us go speak to Hendry," Gavin said as they retrieved their mounts.

It was a short ride to the keep, the entire time they were silent. Gavin went over the details of the day in his mind. There didn't seem to be an easy explanation to what had occurred.

The road between the village and where Edgar lived was well-traveled. He would have to send men to ask as many people as possible if they'd seen anyone.

Riding past the gates, Gavin's attention remained on the task at hand. He could only think of how Hendry would react at being questioned.

"I am starved," Knox stated, stalking into the house after the stable lads fetched their horses.

Gavin felt more tired than hungry, but he wouldn't be able to rest until speaking with Hendry. He directed a guard to go fetch the warrior and went inside.

The great room was empty, so he went to a table near the hearth, allowing the warmth to envelop him.

Knox had made quick work of alerting the kitchen staff for food and soon bowls of steaming stew, bread, and tankards of ale were brought immediately. Seeing the food Gavin gave in to his body's need for sustenance and he joined Knox.

"Someone else must have seen either Edgar or the attackers," Gavin said while chewing. "I will send men out first thing."

There wasn't much more to discuss. Whatever happened

from the time Edgar left the tavern until he was killed, there didn't seem to be a reason for his death.

"It will be a cold winter," Knox said between bites.

Gavin nodded. "I agree."

Just then Cynden entered the room and strolled toward them. "Did ye see him? How did he die?"

Gavin and Knox took turns telling Cynden what they'd seen and how little they'd been able to discover after speaking to people.

They stopped speaking when Hendry entered and walked to the table. The warrior lowered to sit next to Knox.

Hendry was six and twenty, muscular from sword training, and of medium height. He was well-respected by other guardsmen for his abilities in battle and how he seemed to always keep a level head. His shoulder-length brown hair was pulled back and held in place with a leather strap, and he wore a simple tunic, britches, and leather boots.

"What happens? Why was I confined to my quarters?" he asked looking from one of their faces to the other. His brow lowered as he waited for someone to speak.

"Did ye have an argument with a man called Edgar at the tavern earlier today?" Gavin asked.

Hendry shrugged. "Aye, the man was drunk. I made a jest about him smelling of chicken shit. He took offense and hit me on the back of the head with his tankard. Spilled ale all over me, I had to go to the loch and wash. Why are ye asking about that?"

Taking the man in, it seemed as if Hendry wasn't aware of the other man's death.

Gavin met Hendry's gaze. "The man, Edgar, was killed on

his way home. Cut through with a blade."

Hendry's expression barely changed, which was not surprising given he was a warrior. "What does that have to do with me?"

"Did ye kill him?" Gavin asked.

Hendry gave him a droll look. "Nay."

Knox pointed at Hendry with his fork. "When ye left the village to return here, did ye see a group of men near the forest?"

This time Hendry's eyebrows lifted. "Strange ye should ask because I sensed someone watching me. I thought to see some riders in the trees."

Knox seemed puzzled. "Did ye see Edgar on the road?"

Hendry shook his head. "I dinnae and before ye ask. I donnae know where he lives."

"Lived," Gavin said pushing back from the table. "Tomorrow ye will go with us to where ye sensed someone watching. A man who lives along the road where the dead man lived, saw a group of men lingering near the wood's edge."

"Do ye think I killed Edgar?" Hendry asked. Despite his blank expression, from the hardness of his gaze, there was underlying tension.

"Nay," Gavin replied. "I had to ask since ye and he were seen arguing."

"We didnae argue. He stood too close to me. I told him he stank. He hit me with a tankard. That was all."

"Be here in the morning, tell four men to come as well. After first meal we head out," Knox instructed the warrior who stood.

With one last look at Gavin, Hendry frowned. "I would

nae kill a man over something that happens in the tavern."

"I believe ye," Gavin replied. "Dinnae worry yerself."

The warrior shook his head. "Family?"

"Wife, her parents and four bairns," Gavin replied.

Hendry shook his head. "Why would someone kill him? He was nae a fighter."

"That is what we must find out," Knox said.

Gavin ate every bit of the stew, sopping up bits with bread and then he trudged up the stairs and to his bedchamber. He sat to pull off his boots and stockings, followed by his britches and tunic. Once bereft of clothing he washed up and donned a clean tunic.

The bed was welcoming as he fell into it. His mind went to the scene at the dead man's house. The family would mourn for days, the wife longer. It had been obvious the dead man was well-liked and that he'd been a hard worker, ensuring to provide a modest, yet good life for his family.

There was no sense to his death. There didn't seem to be anyone who outwardly hated the man, or anything pointing to him having a grudge with someone. The more Gavin thought about it, the more he grew convinced that Edgar's death had been one of opportunity. He'd been a convenient kill, in the right place without any witnesses.

Rolling to his back he looked up into the darkness. What would he find out the next day? Who and why did someone kill a defenseless man?

THE NEXT MORNING he met with Cynden just before breaking

their fast. Gavin informed his brother that he and the guardsmen would be patrolling in an effort to locate Edgar's killer. The youngest brother brooded at having to remain behind once again.

"Ye should stay here, ye are older and who Alex left in his stead," Cynden stated, his hazel gaze darkening.

"I have begun this and wish to finish," Gavin stated. "Just one day."

Cynden looked toward the great room and Gavin understood. It was not an easy task to help their people with whatever problems they brought before them. Representing the clan was, indeed, a heavy burden.

"Ye will do well in our brother's place," Gavin said meeting Cynden's hazel gaze instantly feeling the strong bond between them.

Cynden's lips curved. "I will rule with an iron fist."

Gavin chuckled. "I know ye will."

After breaking their fast, Gavin, Knox, Hendry, and four additional guardsmen made their way to the courtyard where their horses awaited. As one they mounted to prepare to leave.

He caught sight of a pair of women across the courtyard, at the well. Freya was with the servant girl Flora. They drew water from the well and filled other buckets.

She looked beautiful in the morning light, her raven black tresses braided and wound around her head.

Seeming to sense his regard, she lifted her face and looked to him. Her brow crinkled at noting him being surrounded by the others. All of them armed.

The other lass noticed her watching them and came to stand next to her, both of them searching him and his men as if trying to figure out what happened.

Gavin lifted his hand to them in assurance. Both returned the gesture then turned back to their tasks.

He slid a look to Knox who studied him with an amused look. "She is bonnie."

"Let us go," Gavin ordered, pretending not to have heard his cousin.

IT WAS A sunny day, barely a cloud in the sky, making it easy to see distances. The group of Ross men rode at a gallop to the road leading from the village.

They slowed upon reaching the area where Hendry had sensed being watched. It was not far from the same patch of forest the man they'd spoken to the day before had pointed out. However, it was on a different road.

"Do we know of any groups of men that would need to ride about?" Gavin asked his guards.

The men shook their heads.

"Could be they were rounding up errant herds," one guard offered.

It was possible. However, what didnae make sense is that they would linger along the edge of the woods. Or that they would be together and not spread out to search for the animals.

Knox had been trained by one of the best clan Ross trackers, his father. More times than not, the lairds had relied on the elder or the son to assist with tracking for the lost, whether people or animal.

Since his father's demise, no one could compete with Knox.

"Can ye see if ye can track where they came from?" Gavin asked his cousin.

Gavin and the others rode a horse length behind as Knox guided his steed closer to the trees. He dismounted and bent low studying the ground and plants. After a few moments, he pointed to where there were broken branches.

"A group has recently traveled through. Both humans and horses were here," Knox said and looked at Gavin, who motioned for the others to stay back, then also dismounted.

"Whoever they were they'd either not expected to be seen or were not hiding. Either way because of it, it should be easy to track where the group of men went," Knox informed him.

Both Gavin and Knox remained on foot, guiding the group as they continued forth. Soon, the trail led them to an open field past another line of trees. From where they emerged, it was a clear path to a village that used to be part of Mackinnon hold before Munro took it over.

"Do ye think…" Knox stopped midsentence as they all looked across the expanse of land to the village where people milled about their day-to-day activities.

"Mackinnon warriors." Knox looked from him to the others and then met his gaze once again. In Knox's eyes Gavin saw a myriad of emotions: trepidation, sorrow, and resolve.

"I think the Mackinnon warriors have definitely returned," Gavin said, his blood running cold. "And they seek revenge."

CHAPTER FIVE

"The poor wee ones," Una said to another woman in the laundry. "The smallest will nae remember her father."

They'd spent most of the day ruminating over the death of the man called Edgar, who'd been killed the day before. From what Freya gathered, he and his family were well-liked. Then again people always spoke well of the dead.

"I wonder where the men went today," the other woman said. The question had been repeated several times as everyone questioned if Gavin, Knox, and the others would return with the culprit.

A young lad rushed in, face flushed. "They return!" he yelled. "Mister Gavin returns with all the men." He raced away, probably to inform others.

"Come," Una grabbed Freya's hand. "Let us go see what occurs."

Despite not feeling as if she had any right to be part of what happened in the household, she was curious and allowed the older woman to pull her to the kitchen entrance where many of the servants had already gathered.

A pair of bold chambermaids went so far as to grab buckets and pretend to be fetching water, so they could get a good look to see who returned and hopefully hear what the men spoke about.

Atop his steed, Gavin presented a handsome picture. She could scarcely drag her gaze from him. Jaw set firm, eyes flat, he seemed in a sour mood. When looking to the other men, who'd returned with him, Freya noted they had the same expressions. Whatever they'd discovered it was not good news.

She let out a breath hoping it was not something so bad it would bring more sorrow to the clan.

Flora rushed up to stand beside her. She must have considered the same because she looked to Freya and shook her head.

They went back inside just as Peigi, the cook walked to the kitchen entrance. "Ye all have work to do, time to prepare last meal," she said to her kitchen maids.

Peigi's expression was glum when she turned to Freya. "Will ye help with serving? We are short of help, with two lasses sick."

"Aye, of course," Freya said.

Before she could walk into the kitchen, Peigi stopped her. "Go to the great room and find out when they'd like the meal served."

The woman looked grieved. "Whatever happens, I sense everyone will be in low spirits. I made fruit tarts and sweetened hot mead."

Peigi hurried away into the kitchen and Freya looked to Una who'd joined everyone in the kitchen. "Who should I ask?"

"Lady Ainslie," The woman replied giving her a soft push. "Go on lass. Dinnae tarry."

As Peigi predicted, the great room was quiet. Besides Ainslie, the only ones in the room were Gavin, Cynden, his cousin Knox, and a pair of warriors.

Ainslie sat with Lady Ross, who'd just returned that day. Upon seeing Freya, Ainslie motioned her closer.

Gavin looked up as she entered, his gaze following her progress. Freya kept her eyes downcast, not daring to meet his. It was hard not to look, but she didn't wish to be drawn into whatever sorrow surrounded everyone. She had enough sadness in her own life.

"Peigi wishes to know when ye would like the meal served," Freya said looking from Lady Ross to Ainslie, and dared a glance to see which table the men went to sit at in case Peigi asked.

Lady Ross gave her a curious look. "Ye look much better lass. How do ye fare?"

Caught by surprise that the woman remembered her, Freya took a moment to reply. "I am well. Thank ye, my lady."

"I am glad to hear it," the woman replied. "Tell Peigi to serve some sweetened hot mead. I believe it is needed."

"She is preparing it now." Freya replied.

Lady Ross nodded. "Tell Peigi, the meal can also be served." She looked to where the men sat. "I fear it will be a long night."

Freya hurried from the room and moments later returned, along with another kitchen maid to serve the hot beverages. Most of the men took the cups and drank from them absently.

Gavin, however, looked up and met her gaze. "Thank ye."

There was something in his expression akin to sadness or perhaps worry that made her want to ask questions. Though it was not her place to do so. No matter what the status of her birth, now she was nothing more than a servant at the Ross keep.

ONCE THE MEAL was served, Freya was dismissed and without a reason to linger, she went to her cottage. She carried a tankard of the sweet mead wishing to drink it while she rested. Hopefully the drink would help her sleep.

She'd not needed to ask questions, rumors flew and soon the entire household was aware not only of the way the man Edgar had been horribly attacked and killed.

Instantly images of her own parents' senseless deaths had encompassed Freya almost doubling her with physical pain as sadness enveloped her. She'd never forget the images of them being brought back on the back of a wagon, their bruised and battered lifeless bodies being carried into the house.

Her sweet father had fought as much as he could against the attackers. He'd suffered greatly for it, his face had been unrecognizable.

Freya wiped tears that flowed freely down her face and let out a long breath. She couldn't allow despair to take over. Not now.

Carefully, she placed kindling in the small hearth, adding bits here and there until the fire burned fully, its heat flowing into the room.

Freya sat on her bed and sipped the mead as she pondered what had occurred that day and did it mean more death to come. Certainly with as many men as Clan Ross had, they would soon find those responsible. A shiver went through her and she glanced to the door, once again thankful to be inside the walls of the keep.

It had been pure luck that she and her brother had washed up near Keep Ross and had been given harbor there. Otherwise, Freya wasn't sure where she would have ended up.

The warmth of the mead settled in her stomach as she peered at the fire imagining that she was back home in her bedchamber, her parents in another room, and her brother nearby. It seemed like another lifetime since she'd been home and part of a family.

A tear slipped down her cheek, and she brushed it away. Nothing would bring that life back. It was best not to dwell on the sadness, but to remember the happy moments.

A knock on the front door jolted Freya out of her musings.

Her heartbeat quickened.

Who would come to her door?

Although several of the guards had made crude comments on occasion, none had dared be so bold as to come to her door. At least she hoped not.

She listened intently for a voice, hoping it was Flora or Una. Finally, she stood and went to the door.

"Who is it?"

"Gavin." The reply made her eyes widen.

There was little choice, she had to allow him in. Her hand trembled as she unbolted the door and opened it.

"Is something wrong?" Freya said, her voice breathless. She took a step back, unsure if she should invite him in.

"May I enter?" he asked.

Freya nodded, and he walked in. Immediately the tiny interior seemed even smaller making it hard to keep distance between them.

Gavin's face was etched with lines of exhaustion. He'd pulled the strap that held his shoulder length hair tied back leaving the tresses tussled, which unfortunately was rather flattering. A woman with windblown hair like that would look like a hag, but he looked as if recently ravished.

He lowered to the only chair in the room and looked to the fire. "It has been a hard day." Gavin didn't look at her, his gaze remaining on the flickering flames. It was almost as if he spoke to himself and not her.

Freya retrieved a small cup and poured half of the mead into it. Then she handed it to him. "What happened today?"

For a moment he didn't say anything, then his green gaze lifted to her. "For years we fought battles. Our people have suffered and lost so much. It was supposed to be over."

She nodded. "It is. The Mackinnon is dead."

His chuckle was mirthless. "He is."

"So this attack has something to do with the late laird?" Freya asked not wanting to know the answer, but realizing he wished to talk, to unburden to someone.

Gavin lifted the cup and looked at it as if noticing it for the first time. "I cannae drink this. It is for ye."

"I brought a large tankard of it. I have nae drunk all that I poured for myself."

"Ye are an intelligent lass. Aye, we believe men who were loyal to the late Mackinnon are who may now be attacking our people."

Freya remained silent, her stomach sinking at the news.

He sipped the drink and finally looked to her. "I am nae prepared to stand in my brother's stead. Munro is gone and has his own responsibilities. Cynden is young yet."

"If yer brother believes ye to be the one who will stand in his stead, then ye must. I hear from the staff that ye are a fair and good leader."

His astonished look almost made her smile. "Ye have

heard thus?"

"I have," Freya said nodding. "And what is said in the servant quarters is usually negative."

He let out a long sigh. "Ye should nae be a servant. I know not who ye are, but it is obvious ye are highborn."

"I am here to seek refuge and must pay in some way. I dinnae mind and prefer keeping busy to being left to my thoughts with nothing to do. Una, Flora, and Peigi have been very kind to me."

They were silent for a few moments, it was interesting how comfortable she felt in his presence, despite the flurry of butterflies whenever their gazes met.

"In the past, the fighting brought many times of sorrow. Today, a family grieved the death of a man who did nothing to provoke it," Gavin said with a hard edge to his tone. "We are missing a guard and believe he too was attacked."

Freya thought back to how she and her brother had grieved the death of their parents. The pain had been unbearable. Crushing them. Making it impossible to think clearly or even function. Her heart went to the family who was currently experiencing such a burden.

"Ye know grief well," Gavin stated. "Yer brother died to save ye. It was honorable and yet unfortunate."

"If ye suspect who is responsible, then ye will find them and they will pay," Freya stated, needing to move the conversation away from her own pain. It would be hard to stop crying if she started. There were many things she feared disclosing, so it was best not to begin speaking about her family.

Gavin shook his head. "If my suspicious are correct, then

there are some who dinnae accept Clan Ross as their overseers and seek to avenge their laird's death."

"But he was cruel and unjust," Freya countered. "Why would they remain loyal to such a man?"

"It is nae easy to accept defeat, to become subjects of a clan whom they fought against for a long time. If I am to be honest, this is nae unexpected. We should have been prepared for it."

"Why kill an innocent man?"

"That is what I must find out." He looked at her for a long time and she couldn't tear her eyes away.

His gaze turned hard. "The others have brought up another possibility. One I dinnae like."

Immediately she knew. They'd brought up that perhaps whoever searched for her was taking revenge on Clan Ross for giving her harbor. Freya's mouth turned dry making it impossible to speak.

"Yer secrets are yer own. However, understand that if they bring danger or trouble to our shores, it will be on yer head. Sooner rather than later, ye must talk."

A cold shiver went down Freya's spine. The same man who came to her with his troubles, now looked at her with suspicion.

"I prefer to think of ye as a kind woman. Someone who seeks refuge and will nae repay our amity with treachery or deceit."

When Gavin stood to his full height, again it was as if the room shrunk around them. He was both terrifying and enticing.

Freya got to her feet and met his gaze. "I dinnae feel that my past troubles would ever cause ye hardship. I would flee before allowing anything to affect the kind people of this keep."

"I hope what ye say is true." His expression softened when he looked from her to the door. "I want to believe ye, Freya."

He sought comfort and unable to keep from it, Freya touched Gavin's forearm. When he turned to her, she slipped her arms around his waist and hugged him tight. It wasn't meant to be sensual or provocative. More someone comforting another person, giving them strength and understanding.

After a moment of hesitation, he released a long sigh and returned the hug, pressing his cheek to Freya's temple. Two people, unsure of the future, and sharing the understanding was what they were. Both needed the reassurance the other offered.

"All will be well," Freya said dropping her arms, feeling suddenly utterly sad that he could not remain. How she craved the company of another, sharing thoughts and talking of nothing important.

He gave her one last long look and walked away soon disappearing into the darkness of the courtyard beyond.

For hours, she tossed and turned in bed. The more she considered it, the stranger it was that Gavin had come to her that evening. Surely he could have unburdened himself with either his brothers or his family.

Was there perhaps a lover that he could share all his thought with?

Although she didn't think he had a lover, the thought of a woman with him, made her insides twist. Freya kicked the blankets off and went to the hearth, adding another log. Of all the stupid things she could do, allowing feelings for a man to grow, would be the worst.

After all, it had been emotions—thinking herself in love—that had been the catalyst for the demise of her entire family. Her parents and brother were dead because she'd been blind to what was clearly in front of her.

Gavin's words of it being on her head were true, and terrifying. The burdens she brought with her from the past were already unbearable, she could never bear bringing troubles to more people.

Despite the words she'd uttered, her betrothed was a ruthless man who cared for no one but himself. He was capable of murder, of killing whoever stood in his path. Perhaps she should tell Gavin everything and let him decide if she should go away.

At thoughts of Tasgall Macgregor, fear overtook, and she began to shiver. Was he coming for her? Was he already there and killing whoever didn't tell him where she was?

Knowing she'd be unable to sleep, Freya poured water from a pitcher into the pot that hung on a hook, added herbs and swung it over the fire to simmer.

As she watched the flames, she considered what to do. She had only managed to save a few coins. To be able to afford to travel elsewhere and scratch out the beginnings of a meager existence, she needed another several month's worth of wages. Then she could buy fare and head to a place far away.

One thing was certain, she could not remain in the same place for long.

CHAPTER SIX

Instead of going to first meal, Gavin stalked out of the house via one of the rear doorways. In his current sour mood it was best to avoid conversations until he had the opportunity to clear his head.

All night he'd tossed and turned. Thoughts of Freya and how frail she'd looked after his statement. He'd felt guilty at having threatened her, so much so that he'd almost gone back to her. Then there was the situation with Edgar's death and the missing guard. People would be demanding to know who was responsible.

If his and Knox's suspicions were right, the clan's people would be plunged into panic again. In his heart Gavin knew that the period of peace was short-lived and once again they had to plan for battle.

He walked without a destination toward the seashore, the soft sounds of the lapping waves immediately soothing his chaotic mind. Standing with feet apart and arms to his sides, he closed his eyes and inhaled deeply.

Opening his eyes, he looked to the peaceful surroundings. In the distance, fishermen pushed small boats out into the water, others were already out sitting in place casting nets. It was a beautiful land where he lived. Lush green pastures, the grayish blue waters of the sea, and the gently sloping hills butting up against jagged higher ones upon which goats and sheep grazed.

This day they'd ride out to what used to be Mackinnon lands, first they'd speak with Munro and then they'd begin the task of setting a trap for the attackers.

When his stomach growled, he turned to head back to the keep but hesitated at catching sight of Freya walking along the shoreline.

She'd not seen him, which allowed him a candid view of her as she walked slowly, head bent. He smiled when the waves lapped at her ankles, and she hurried away as the chilly waters touched her bare skin.

Bending, she picked up something and studied it, then she continued forth toward him. Seeming to sense him, she looked up and her eyes widened. "I didnae expect anyone to be out here so early."

Gavin pushed hair out of his eyes. "I could nae sleep."

For a moment she studied him. "I was restless as well." She peered toward the house. "I do nae have to work until later today," she explained.

"I am glad," Gavin replied. "What do ye plan to do?"

Her shoulders lifted and lowered. "Since I could nae sleep, I made a list. First walk along the shore. Then I will pick some flowers for my bedside table. I will join the others for the midday meal and then help with mending."

Gavin wanted to remain there with her. To continue talking to her was preferable to what his day would entail. Then again, he considered talking with Freya preferable to most things.

"It sounds like a full day," he said.

For a moment they stood in silence, seeming as though neither wished to walk away. It was almost as if she felt the same pull toward him that he did toward her.

Although Gavin considered, it was probably wishful thinking on his part. She was a beautiful woman who'd surely had love interests in the past. Perhaps she was involved with someone and waited for him to come for her.

"Freya…" he said and stopped.

She looked up at him, the dark gaze meeting his, locking with his. It was as if time stood still. He reached for her hand glad when she didn't pull away. It was cool and delicate.

"What is it?" she asked in a hoarse whisper. There was something pleading in her gaze.

"Tell me something. Anything. About ye."

Her lips parted. When she tried to pull her hand away, he held it fast. "Why are ye so afraid?"

The way her eyes traveled to his lips, made his heart thunder. He wanted this woman and if not careful, she could very well steal his heart.

"I-I do not wish to bring ye more troubles…"

He bent closer until their faces almost touched. "Freya."

For a moment he thought she'd kiss him, their lips but a hair's breadth apart. "I wish I could."

Yanking her hand away, she turned and walked away.

Gavin followed her progress as she went in the direction she'd come, once again studying the shoreline.

As soon as the issues with Edgar's murder were investigated and a culprit or culprits found, there would be no more delays when it came to Freya.

She would be given no choice in the matter. Freya would

have to tell them everything.

Looking up to the sky, he hoped she was not tied to another man.

AS EXPECTED MUNRO was aggrieved at learning what had occurred, but like them he'd no idea who would agree to join a band of men who would wish to become targets of Clan Ross, especially now that they were at a huge disadvantage.

"A trap could work," Munro stated as they walked to the edge of the surrounding forest near the keep where he lived. They looked across the fields to where the village of Armadale was. It was a large bustling village, almost twice the size of Tokavaig, which made it difficult to pin down who would be part of the warrior force for the late laird.

Additionally, people still didn't fully trust Clan Ross. Despite Munro working toward garnering the trust of the local people, it could take years to actually acquire their full allegiance.

Not surprisingly, there were the residual few who held a grudge against anyone affiliated with their clan.

As it stood, the people of Armadale had learned over years of mistreatment to depend only on one another. They would never turn on their own.

"We have started patrolling the lands near where the attack happened," Gavin stated. "In pairs of two."

Munro gave him a puzzled look. "It could prove dangerous, especially if there are six of them."

"True," Gavin said. "We have to draw them out somehow.

They will nae come out against a larger contingency."

"What if we disguise one guard as a villager. Have guards hidden nearby," Knox suggested.

Munro shook his head. "That would be too dangerous as well."

He let out a long sigh. "I dinnae wish to have to send a message to Alexander. I must let him know. He has to be informed."

They continued coming up with different plans, only to discard idea after idea. Wishing to continue their patrol, Gavin and his men left Munro's home, deciding to ride through Armadale and get a sense of the people there.

As they rode down the center of the village, a woman rushed out from her home and hurried her children into the house. Conversations stopped and wary gazes watched in silence, some with ill-disguised hatred.

Most of the people they came across did not look to be warriors. Gavin studied faces, attempting to recognize features. Unfortunately, because he was an archer, it meant he'd rarely been up close during battles. He referred to the other men, hoping they'd be better at seeing someone they'd once fought against.

When leaving the village, it had become obvious how hard it would be to find whoever the attackers were.

EACH OF THE following days, Gavin and several guards questioned people, but nothing came of it. The more days that passed, the more frustrated everyone became.

On a good note, there were no other attacks. However, he dreaded going to see Edgar's family and inform them he'd been unsuccessful in finding the culprit.

The missing guard had not returned, which was still cause for concern. Either he'd left on his own accord, or he was injured.

It was late afternoon, thankfully there hadn't been many grievances that day. Perhaps because there was a steady drizzle all day, which tended to keep most indoors or near their homes.

He'd not seen Freya in a pair of days, so he called to the servant Flora as she entered the great room. The lass came to where he stood looking up at him with curiosity.

"Is Freya continuing to work in the laundry?" he asked, looking from her to the corridor that led to where the kitchens and laundry rooms were.

"Aye, she is. She also helps in the kitchens when Peigi needs help," Flora said following his line of sight with a worried expression of pinched brows. "She is a good worker, she really is."

Gavin tried to soften his expression. "I am only asking because I had nae seen her."

The lass visibly relaxed. "She prefers to remain away from the main rooms, sir."

Several thoughts occurred to him. Was Freya afraid someone would recognize her? Or did she stay away because she wished to avoid being questioned?

He could visit her again in the evening. True it had been uncharacteristic of him to go to her. Especially as he wasn't sure to trust her.

As much as he tried to deny it internally, there was more than just needing to know her past. He was attracted to Freya. An attraction so strong that it could cloud his judgement when it came to finding out if she brought danger to his home.

Alexander had left it up to him to deal with Freya's situation and he would never purposely falter in his duties. At the same time, a strong sense of protecting Freya filled him whenever he was near her.

There was no putting it off. He had to speak to her and find out the truth. Not only because it was his duty, but because he yearned to know her better, know more about the mysterious woman.

A commotion from the entrance yanked Gavin from his musings as guards rushed in with an injured warrior. The man's arms were draped across the other's shoulders, his feet dragging across the stone floor, leaving a trail of blood.

Gavin jumped to his feet and rushed to help them lift the moaning man onto a table.

"Fetch the healer," someone called out and people raced in different directions. Some toward the kitchens for bandaging and water, others to get out of the way.

It was the missing guard.

The injured man was called Gerard, he was an archer. Face scrunched in pain, he held out a hand and Gavin grabbed it. "Who did this?"

"M-MacKinnons," he stuttered and passed out.

"Was anyone with him?" Gavin asked the men who'd brought Gerard in.

Both shook their heads. "Nay he said to be heading away from his family's home when attacked. They near the western coast," one man explained.

Just then the healer came in, obviously the man had been at the keep already, which was fortunate.

Knox walked in and touched Gavin's shoulder. "We must hurry and ride out. Perhaps someone saw this happen."

"Aye, I agree, but his injuries look old. He was probably attacked a day or two ago. I suspect, the cowards are much too clever to attack in plain sight."

As Gavin headed to the stairwell to fetch his weapons, he caught sight of Freya walking into the great room with an armload of bandages. She hesitated at seeing him, their eyes clashing for a moment before she looked to the injured guard. Freya paled, her expression turning sorrowful.

It was obvious, to him at least, that Gerard would probably not survive the injuries.

He would have to question Freya another day.

No one had seen anything. The area where the injured man had been found was remote, no houses for miles. The area was far from where Edgar had been attacked.

"They must have attacked him on the main road here," Knox said, looking around.

They'd stopped by Gerard's home and informed his family, who immediately headed to the keep. They confirmed that he'd visited and left two days earlier. No one had seen or heard anything after he'd gone.

The family lived near the shore, the nearest neighbor was far and not on the way toward the keep. Still they questioned the people who told them not to have seen anything or noticed any men riding past.

Now as they found a place where it was obvious someone had been hurt, by the dark pools of blood and broken low branches, fury engulfed Gavin.

"They are cowards to attack lone men, leaving them for dead," He uttered past a clenched jaw.

"It is fortunate the men on patrol found him," a guard said. The gruff man cleared his throat. "If he survives, that is."

A strange sense of being watched made Gavin turn toward a small grouping of trees in the distance. He pointed. "They could be hiding there."

They road toward the trees, but upon reaching the area, there was no one about. Just past the trees was a thicker forest line.

"This is where they had to come from." Gavin was sure the same group had been lurking about, waiting for any opportunity to attack.

Still he could not shake the sense that someone had recently been there. "Knox, look about."

Knox had already dismounted and was inspecting the area. "Aye, more than one has been through here."

Gavin stomach clenched. "The bastards came far into Ross lands. How is it possible that no one has seen them?"

"Threats," one warrior stated. "People may be afraid to speak."

"No," Gavin said. "They are proficient in hiding. Whoever they are, are seasoned warriors. Men bent on revenge."

CHAPTER SEVEN

As the heavy bucket of water appeared from the well, Freya took it and poured the water into another one. It was the second of three trips and already her arms grew weary.

Still, she was proud. Upon first arriving, she'd barely been able to get the bucket up, much less carry two into the house.

Once the second one was full, she reached for a handle, only to stop when a masculine hand wrapped around it.

"I'll take them inside for ye." A man she recognized as Hendry, gave her a flirty look. "Ye work too hard, Freya."

So he knew her name. Before she could protest, he lifted the buckets as if they weighed no more than a feather and began walking toward the house as she awkwardly strode alongside.

"Ye dinnae have to do this. Fetching water is part of my duties." Freya had to scamper to keep up with his long strides.

Upon reaching the laundry, the two women in the room looked up. Flora's face brightened. "Pour it into here," she said pointing to a large basin.

When he placed one down to do as Flora instructed, Freya took the opportunity to grab the other one and pour it into the basin as well.

"Thank ye," she said grabbing the buckets and rushing back outside, while praying he had something to do in the house and would not follow.

Apparently, her prayers went unanswered when he caught up to her. "Flora said ye had one more trip."

Setting her back teeth, she nodded. "Aye, but I can do it. I am sure ye have duties to attend to."

He shrugged. "I am waiting for the others, so we do target practice. No one is there as yet." Hendry glanced toward the open field. "Ye are a bonnie lass, Freya," he said casually. "Do ye have a husband?"

Immediately the thought of Tasgall came to mind. The man she'd fallen in love with and who'd betrayed her entire family. "I am nae interested in marriage."

The comment didn't seem to put a damper on the attractive warrior's mood. Instead he gave her a broad smile. "Ah, so ye have yer eye on someone then?"

Despite her annoyance at the man's flirting, there was something about him that set her at ease and curiosity got the best of her. "How did ye come to that conclusion?"

"I am a tracker and a warrior. It makes me very good at seeing more than what a person states."

"Is that so?" Freya couldn't help teasing him.

"Hendry." The deep familiar voice caught them both off guard. Neither had noticed Gavin's approach.

Something fluttered in Freya's stomach at seeing the wickedly handsome man. His green gaze took them in as if regarding an interesting object. His expression was impassive, but she noticed a slight flex of his jaw.

"Gavin," Hendry replied while pouring water into the second bucket. "I am helping this fair lass while waiting for everyone to come."

The green gaze moved from Hendry to the buckets and lastly to her. "Freya, ye should nae be carrying heavy buckets of water."

It was ridiculous. There she stood with two huge men, both acting as if she were some sort of frail woman who could barely walk without assistance.

She bent to grab the buckets. When both reached toward them, she glared up at them. "I am fully capable of performing my duties without assistance from either of ye."

Admittedly, since Hendry had filled the buckets to the brim, they were heavier, but she managed to lift them without wobbling and despite her arms protests, she rushed away.

A grin spread across her face upon entering the dim interior where she stopped and put the heavy buckets down. It had been a long time since she'd garnered the attention of more than one man.

"I do believe our lass has an admirer or two," Flora told the other laundress. "Did ye see how Hendry looked at her?"

Freya rolled her eyes unable to keep from smiling. "I am sure he was just being helpful."

"When have ye seen Hendry in the laundry?" Flora asked and both she and the other woman shook their heads. "Never," both said in unison.

At meal break, Flora suggested they take their food out to the side of the house where they could watch the archers practice.

There was a sturdy table with benches for the servants to use. Already a pair of chambermaids sat there watching the practice.

"He is handsome," Flora said when Hendry walked up to

take his turn. "Do ye fancy him?"

"Nae," Freya said and added upon Flora's incredulous look, "I do think he is an attractive man."

He'd mentioned archery practice and wondered if it meant Gavin would participate as well.

She sipped from her bowl of soup while looking on as several archers shot at the targets. Her question was answered when Gavin approached the marked spot and lifted his bow. In her opinion, no other man could compete with him when it came to looks. By the rapt attention of the other women, they agreed.

One of the chambermaids let out a dramatic sigh causing the other one to giggle.

Flora clasped her hands dramatically against her chest mimicking a swoon. Despite herself Freya chuckled.

Gavin looked toward the giggling group of chambermaids and frowned. Apparently he lost concentration because he completely missed the target. This made the other archers clear their throats in an effort not to laugh.

INSTEAD OF JOINING Flora and the others for the evening meal, Freya wished to be alone that evening.

It was a quiet day. Someone stated that it could be because Laird Ross was returning. The thought made Freya want to hide, lest he see her and demand answers to the same questions of her past.

In the mood to cook, she gathered two small potatoes, pieces of leftover ham, some cream, and a small onion from the kitchen and carried the items to her cottage.

Once inside, she washed the vegetables and then cut the

potatoes and the onion, she hummed recalling the many days she'd asset the cook at her home on Eigg. She put the chopped vegetables into a small pot, added the ham and cream, along with water, to make the potato soup that she'd been craving.

While the meal cooked, she poured water into a basin and then stripped. As she washed her body and then hair.

Her weekly ritual of bathing had been so very different before. Servants had filled her wooden tub with heated water and fragrant oils. She'd luxuriated in the water until it became cool and had assistance to wash her waist-long hair.

Now she kneeled on the floor and with a chipped cup poured water over her hair the water dripping into a small basin.

Once bathed and having donned her nightshift, she sat near the small hearth drying her hair and eating the flavorful soup. She was glad that as pampered as her life had been, her mother had insisted they learn the basics of cooking and sewing. Otherwise, she would have been at a horrible disadvantage.

With only one night shift and two changes of clothing, she'd already had to mend the skirts several times.

The next day, she was to go to the village with Una and she planned to purchase some inexpensive fabric to make herself another nightshift and perhaps a blouse to wear under her vest.

After rinsing her bowl and cup, she went to the door to toss the dirty water out.

The courtyard was quiet, only a pair of guards walking about. More guards had been sent out to patrol since the attacks and Freya was glad to live within the walls of the keep.

Movement caught her attention, and she realized it was Gavin wearing a cloak. He went to the guards, and they stood in a circle talking. He carried the weight of lairdship in his brother's absence well, and yet Freya imagined it was quite a heavy burden.

In the early mornings, she caught sight of him riding out to patrol. In the afternoon, he sat in the great room to preside over lairdship duties, then he practiced. And now, after last meal, he checked on the men.

Interesting that she'd not noticed if his brother, Alexander, had also done the same. She imagined he did.

Seeming to sense her, he looked toward where she stood, and Freya's stomach dipped. There she stood like a dolt in nothing more than a nightshirt with wet hair. Although partially hidden by the door, she was sure he saw her.

He turned back to the men, continuing the conversation. Freya took the opportunity to toss out the second bucket of water, then closed the door.

First at archery practice and now again he caught her watching him. The man no doubt thought her to be enamored of him. She should have dashed back inside and not watched for so long.

She wasn't surprised when two raps on the door sounded.

Letting out a breath she cracked the door open and looked up at him.

"Is there something bothering ye, Freya?" He took her in with a blank expression.

"Bo-bothering me? Nae. Wh-why do ye ask?" She was stammering like an idiot. "I was just tossing water out."

"Ye should nae be outside with no clothes on." A smile

played at the corner of his lips. "It could bring ye unwanted attention."

"Are ye the guardian of all women then?" Freya snapped. Why did he think she needed his advice? If anything, why was he here now?

His eyes slid to the side. "Ye have been quite fiery today. A temper in a lass is very appealing."

Freya opened her mouth, then closed it. Before thinking of his status, she slammed the door in his face. Immediately, her breath caught, and she gasped at what she'd done.

Yanking the door open, she found him still standing in the same place, both eyebrows raised in surprise.

"I-I should nae have done that." She said waiting for what he'd say.

His gaze traveled down her body, and she fought not to move behind the door. "I will leave ye to rest," he said not moving.

"Is there more news?" Freya asked not wanting him to leave. "About the attacks."

He shook his head. "Nae. The patrols have nae been fruitful. I can only hope tomorrow brings something."

She nodded meeting his gaze. "I will pray that it does."

When he leaned forward, Freya was sure he would kiss her. How she wanted him to. Without thinking of it, her eyes fluttered shut of their own accord.

The soft press of his lips still took her by surprise, her entire body came to life.

Before she could return the kiss, it was over. Heat surged up her chest to her face as her eyes flew open.

Gavin backed away, his eyes on her. "Sleep well, Freya."

"Oh goodness," she closed the door firmly, and slumped against it.

"That should nae have happened," she whispered. "Why had she not stepped away?"

The answer was clear, she'd wanted him to kiss her. Had invited it. At the thought her hands flew to her mouth. "Is that why he'd kissed her? Because she'd closed her eyes? It could be he'd meant to whisper something.

Once again Freya yanked the door open, this time she tentatively stepped out and peered toward the house. Gavin stood a short distance away looking up at the sky.

He turned to her and looked around, then walked back. "What are ye doing? It is cold and ye are nae dressed." He took her by the shoulders pushing her through the doorway. He remained outside the threshold.

"I have to ask," Freya said, sure her face as bright red. "Why did ye kiss me?"

At first he frowned then seeming to realize she required a reply, he gave her an incredulous look. "Because I have wanted to kiss ye for a long time. I should nae, but I want to kiss ye again."

"Ye should nae."

"I am aware," he pressed the tip if his finger to her nose. "Close the door and stay inside."

He pulled the door closed and this time Freya latched it and let out a long breath. His reply should have made her feel better. Instead worry took the place of embarrassment. There could not be anything between them.

The past had proven that allowing emotions free reign would only lead to heartbreak and sorrow.

THANKFULLY, THE FOLLOWING day was sunny. The breeze added a briskness to the day as Freya and Flora sat on the back of a wagon headed toward the village.

They perused the stalls in the village square, not purchasing anything as neither could afford more than the fabric they'd come for. And perhaps something to eat.

A slender woman had greeted them warmly in the fabric shop, where several young women in the back of the room barely acknowledged them as they continued sewing. Apparently, the owner of the shop knew Flora's family because she asked about them.

As they chatted, Freya looked through the more inexpensive fabrics. Lifting the edge of a cream fabric considering it would be perfect for a shift. She gazed longingly toward some beautiful softer materials, knowing they were much too expensive.

Just then movement outside the window caught her attention. People meandered past, women on their way to the market square to purchase items for the evening meal. Men stood outside the tavern talking much too loudly, proof they'd drank too much for the early hour.

A pair of men on horseback brought their horses to a stop outside the window and dismounted. The hairs on the back of her neck rose. Freya's eyes rounded and her breath seized.

The ground seemed to shift under her feet.

She looked around fearing Flora would notice she'd lost interest in the fabric that she gripped with both hands her gaze locked on the men through the window.

One she didn't recognize, but the other was very familiar. He was from Eigg; she was sure of it. He'd worked for her family at the stables.

Why was he there? Was it possible Tasgall was as well? People often traveled between the Isles, however, the man outside was married and neither he nor his wife ever left Eigg.

Breathing became labored and Freya's hands shook as she pondered what to do. She and Flora were to go to the village square after this to wander about the stalls and there would be no way to dissuade her friend. They'd have to walk past the tavern to do so.

Why had she not remained at the keep? It had been foolish to come there where anyone could see her.

Flora continued to talk to the shopkeeper totally unaware of Freya's despair.

Outside, the men pulled their horses behind as they walked in the direction of the village square.

"I have to return to the keep," Freya said, her voice quavering. "I am feeling quite unwell."

"Ye do look pale. All the color has left yer face." Flora took her arm. "Perhaps ye should sit for a bit."

"Is there any way for me to get back?" Freya insisted, not allowing Flora to pull her toward a chair. "I really must go."

Her friend gave her a worried look. "I believe to have seen a pair of guards when we were walking here. Stay here, let me see if I can find them."

Flora dashed from the shop leaving her standing by the doorway, too scared to look out.

"Here drink this," the shop owner said pushing a cup into her hand. "Ye really do look about to faint."

It was not much later that the door opened. Freya's heart began pounding as she prayed that it wasn't one of the men from Eigg. She kept her gaze downcast as she waited for whoever it was to speak to the shop owner.

"Freya," Gavin said as he neared. "Flora says ye feel unwell."

OF ALL THE people to be there, why did it have to be him? Flora hated to lie to him yet again. In truth, her stomach was tumbling, and she did feel as if to faint, so perhaps it wasn't a total lie.

He studied her then looked to Flora. "I will take her back."

She tuned to Flora. "I am so sorry to leave ye."

Flora shrugged. "Dinnae worry. I will get fabric for both of us. Ye like the cream one?"

For some reason her friend's kindness brought tears and she nodded.

"Here." Gavin took several coins from his purse and gave them to a wide-eyed Flora. "To pay for the fabric, both yers and hers."

Flora grinned. "Thank ye."

"Come." He took her elbow, and when she hesitated at the doorway, he mistook the action for her losing the ability to walk. Lifting her into his arms, Gavin carried her to his horse that stood just outside the shop.

"Can ye stand?" he asked.

Freya nodded despite her knees feeling like liquid from being held in such an intimate manner. He mounted and then hoisted her up to sit in front.

The entire ride from the village, Freya kept her face down whilst scanning out of the corner of her eyes for the men. Thankfully, Gavin rode in the opposite direction from which the men had gone.

Upon leaving the village, she let out a breath of relief. There was still the chance the men would come to the keep; she'd have to come up with an excuse to remain away from being seen for the next few days.

"Ye were shaking as if afraid. What occurred?" Gavin asked.

His astuteness was invaluable as a warrior, Freya realized. However, it made it hard to keep things from him. She had to be extremely careful in what she said because Freya had a feeling he'd see through lies.

"I was afraid of becoming ill and poor Flora would have to find a way to help me back to the keep. Now I do nae wish to be sick in front of ye." Freya prayed for forgiveness for all the lies she told.

Leaning back against his chest, with his strong arms around her was much more intimate than she'd ever wished to be after the kiss from the night before.

There was no denying that she was attracted to Gavin Ross.

No, she was more than attracted. She wanted him. Desired him.

If only things were different. If they'd met under different circumstances, two people coming across one another, neither encumbered by duties or a horrible past, she'd be relishing this moment.

Instead she hoped he'd remain unaware of the intensity of her desires.

The horse left the main road and Gavin led it to a wooded area. Flora tensed. "Where are we going?"

"There have been attacks on this road and I noticed a pair of riders left the village behind us. They couldn't see us past the last bend, so I would rather be safe and hide here until they ride past."

Her blood went cold. Could it be the two men from Eigg?

"Yes we should hide," she said attempting to look around him to see the road.

He helped her to dismount and did the same. He guided the horse to a tree away from sight and tethered it. "Stay with him. If I donnae return, mount and ride toward the setting sun. Ye will get to the keep."

"Ye must return," Freya said looking around. It was dense and she couldn't see the sky past the thick trees. "Which way?"

Gavin pointed and she nodded. "Be with care."

Standing next to the horse Freya waited, whilst Gavin bent at the waist and hurried back to the edge of the woods, disappearing within seconds.

"Well, this is turning out to be the most unsettling day," Freya told the huge horse, who lowered its head and began to nibble on newly sprouted grass.

She strained to hear, but other than the wind through the leaves and birdsong, there were no other sounds.

What if the men who'd been behind were the ones from the Isle of Eigg? If they headed to Ross keep, God help her. Or what if they were the attackers? They could kill Gavin.

Freya pulled the small dagger Gavin had gifted her and held it in her right hand while peering in the direction Gavin had gone.

THERE WAS MOVEMENT and she stepped behind the horse, then

peered around it. Gavin appeared and walked toward her.

"They must have gone another way. They've yet to appear. We will wait a bit longer before continuing, just to be safe."

She let out a breath and returned the dagger to the folds of her skirt. Gavin's lips curved. "Ye were prepared to defend yerself. That is good."

Freya gave him a droll look. "I doubt it would have done much good."

He studied her. "Keep it hidden until yer attacker is close enough not to see it. Then strike."

Freya remained silent.

"Do ye still feel unwell?" Gavin studied her, immediately the desire for him returned.

Freya had to drag her gaze from his. "I-I feel better." She almost asked that he return and make sure the men were not headed to Ross keep. Instead, she lifted an unsteady hand and pushed hair from her face. "Did the men seem unfamiliar?"

He shook his head. "I could nae get a good look. They were too far."

The attacks were something to be wary of, which meant most of the Ross guards rode in pairs. It had been unwise for them to have headed to the keep alone.

"I am sorry, this is my fault. We should have waited for the others. I could have stayed inside the seamstress' shop until everyone was ready to leave."

She'd been so shaken by seeing someone from her home isle, she'd not thought clearly. Now because of her, it was possible that Gavin was in danger.

"There is nae need to fret. I will get ye back to the keep." He looked toward the road. "I am glad ye feel better."

Freya walked around the horse stopping not realizing how close he'd stood in front of it. Her mind went blank, too many emotions assaulted at once. "I dinnae know what I am going to do. I have nowhere to go."

"There is something wrong isn't there?" Gavin asked, lifting her chin.

Instead of a reply, she threw herself against him and began to sob.

To her surprise, he rubbed her back in an effort to comfort her. It had the opposite effect, and she began to cry harder.

"Talk to me, Freya," he asked in a soft voice. "Tell me why ye cry."

If the men were from Eigg, and they headed to Ross keep her secret would be discovered. All they had to do was describe her. Freya wasn't sure what to do. If she asked Gavin to help her escape, would he? Or would he hand her over to them, believing whatever lies they told?

"It is just that I am nae sure what to do anymore. I feel as if everything is against me."

With gentle fingers lifted her face. "Is someone threatening ye?"

Self-preservation, she learned, was her only ally. "Nae. It is that I have no one to care about me. Whether I live or die will nae matter one bit. If those men who are killing people kill us, yer family would mourn for ye. For me..." she left the sentence unfinished.

She had family on Eigg, they probably had already mourned her death, thinking both she and Beathan had succumbed at sea. Did they even know what occurred? Her father's brother lived a day's ride away and only visited once a season.

They'd attended her parents' burial. Her uncle had left convinced Beathan would take over the management of the house and lands and that Freya would marry Tasgall. In their minds, all was well.

If she died it could be a long time before her remaining family would be aware, if at all.

Her chest tightened with guilt at not telling Gavin the truth. That she feared the men in the village searched for her.

She gripped the front of Gavin's tunic pulling him closer. "I want to forget everything. I wish to not think of my past or the present. I want to wake up and find that this has all been a dream."

When his mouth crashed over hers, Freya wanted to cry with relief.

For them to come together was inevitable. Since the first time she'd seen Gavin Ross, the pull to him had been strong.

This moment, this time was in all probability the only time for them to have an opportunity to be together. She could not let it pass.

She threw her arms around his neck and raked her fingers through the silky tresses pulling him tight against her, wanted to drink him in. He tasted of ale and promise, and she closed her eyes wishing to commit the taste of him to memory.

Gavin deepened the kiss, his tongue pushing past her parted lips to taste her. Heat traveled from her arms and up her legs to the very center of her being. Sensations like she'd never felt overtook everything blocking out sounds other than each other's breathing and the sounds of their mouths as they continued to kiss.

"Mmmmm," Freya murmured, wanting more. No other

thought could form than need and desire for the man in her arms.

His lips traveled from her mouth down the side of her jaw to her throat. He licked a path, heated breath forming a trail over the sensitive skin. She gripped his wide shoulders throwing her head back to give more access to his mouth. Gavin suckled the side of her neck making her legs go weak.

Her inner fire raged, the flames all consuming. Raking her fingers through his long hair, Freya did her best to convey what she urgently needed by pushed her hips against him.

By the feel of his hardness pulsing against her stomach Gavin wanted her just as fiercely.

"I want ye so much," Gavin whispered against her ear, his hot breathy words fanning the flames of her desire.

"I want ye," Freya replied, turning his face to her and taking his mouth with hers in a kiss that bordered on savage. Their teeth clashed, tongues swirled in a dance of passion.

They lowered to the ground, while continuing to kiss. Gavin pushed her to lay on the soft grass.

His eyes were dark with desire, his mouth swollen from her kisses as he came over her. Then once again he took her mouth with his.

Running her hands up his back, Freya could feel the hard muscles responding to her touch. He was so perfect, everything from his face to his corded body that was oh so very desirable.

"I need ye," Freya rasped out. "I need to know I am alive. To feel fully alive."

He was nuzzling her neck, his teeth raking down the side. "Ye are upset. Ye may regret it."

Oh, God! Freya feared he would stop. Believe she was overcome with emotions and not thinking clearly.

She took his face with both hands and peered into his darkened eyes. "I have never been so sure of anything. Ye must be mine, even if only once."

For a long moment, he met her gaze. The corners of his lips curved into a wicked smile. Her insides threatened to melt from the heat that grew with even more intensity.

"I have wanted ye each night." Each word was accentuated by a push of his hips, the hardness between his legs sliding between hers.

Tingles of anticipation mingled with something new pulsed through her and Freya's breath caught.

Taking her mouth once again, Gavin pushed her skirts up then unfasted the front of his breeches to free himself.

Freya lost any need to be coy, she wanted to touch every inch of him, first she slid her hand over his taut bottom, loving the feel of the soft skin over the hard mounds.

The cool air blew over her exposed skin as the ties of her blouse fell apart when Gavin pulled the end of the strip with his teeth. Immediately his mouth took the tip of one breast in, and he suckled greedily.

"Oh!" Freya bit her bottom lip to keep from crying out.

As he continue to lavish his attention on her breasts, his mouth taking on one then the other, his fingers slipped up her leg and to between the folds of her sex. The tip of his fingers circled the bud between her legs over and over until Freya lost control, her legs moving of their own accord, hips pulsing up into his hand.

Freya pushed her mouth against his throat to muffle her

moans. With each movement of his hand, shocks of pleasure surged until she couldn't withstand it and came with so much force that she thought she might lose consciousness.

As her pleasure ebbed, he began to push into her. Freya wanted all of him, she grabbed his bottom urging him to fill her.

Ever so slowly, with measured movements, he pushed into her. It was the most wonderful feeling, to finally have this man as hers.

Even if for a fleeting moment, this was a time when nothing else existed, but her and him. Their bodies joining in the most intimate of manners.

When he began to move, thrusting in, filling her, expanding her completely, then pulling out just far enough to push back in, Freya began climbing again.

She lifted her hips to match his movements, wanting more, needing to lose control while at the same time not wanting it to end.

His mouth crashed over hers, as he did his best to keep his sounds to a minimum, the throaty moans as enticing as his body.

Thrusting her hands under his tunic, Freya slid her hands up and down his back, digging her fingers into the hard planes. How she wished for them to be without the encumberment of clothing to feel his body against hers.

Gavin's movements became faster, his thrusts harder and Freya threw her head back, lips parted as she gasped for breath.

"Faster… aye… aye." Freya's hoarse whispers filled her own ears.

Plunging harder and faster, Gavin's breathing became labored. His body seeming to have taken on a life of its own. With each thrust Freya climbed higher toward a realm she'd never been, until suddenly it was as if her entire being shattered.

Her cries were muffled as she pushed her face into his shoulder, whilst raking her nails down his back.

His body trembled, Gavin's moan was almost guttural. Suddenly he pulled out completely spilling his seed onto the ground between her legs then collapsing atop her.

Freya clung to him, their hard breathing the only sound in the now quiet woods.

Squeezing her eyes shut, Freya refused to return to reality, instead she imagined the moment would last forever and that she'd wake up to a life where she'd wake up to him next to her every morning.

Gavin rolled form her to lay on the soft grass. He stared up at the sky, seeming to be in thought.

If he uttered that it had been a mistake, Freya was sure her heart would break into a thousand pieces. She held her breath daring a glance at him.

He was flushed, his tussled hair across his cheek.

About to state they should go, Freya opened her mouth only to remain silent when his hand took hers.

For a long moment, they remained on the ground, not speaking.

Finally Gavin rolled to his side and faced her. He cupped her face and pressed a kiss to her forehead and then lips. "I am honored."

Unsure what to say, Freya met his gaze. "It was wonderful."

Gavin's lips curved. "Aye it was." Then he became serious. "We should go."

Instead of standing, he pulled her into his arms and held her close.

Freya was sure once they returned to the keep, they would also return to their former ways.

This moment would be etched in her mind as the most beautiful to have experienced.

Her daydream had been wonderful.

A life that would never—could never—be hers.

CHAPTER EIGHT

WHAT HAD HE done?

Stupid. Stupid.

Did he feel badly about what had occurred between him and Freya?

Did he have regrets?

He did not was the answer to both questions.

It went against every instinct to even consider that making love to Freya was wrong.

Each moment had been beyond belief. It had been the best lovemaking he'd ever experienced. He should not sully it by even considering it as a bad decision.

However, it had been.

That it felt almost impossible to take her again, proved it even more.

He was on his back with his arms around the beautiful woman. Everything in him was unwilling to release her, even though she'd suggested twice already that they should go.

It was true, someone could happen upon them. If it was the men who were attacking the people of Clan Ross, it would prove deadly. And yet.

The woman he held was like no other and in that moment he vowed to protect her up until his last breath.

Was he in love? No, he wasn't so naïve to think that because the interlude had been so powerful, it meant more than it had. The desire they'd both felt for one another was the reason their physical interaction had been so powerful.

Then again, he'd desired women before. Some he'd wanted so much he'd physically ached. Yes, he had enjoyed the bedding. But curiously, he'd never felt as satisfied as he did in that very moment.

What was it about Freya? Why did this woman call to his every instinct, every thought and every part of him?

She lifted her head and pushed up to sit on the ground, next to him fumbling with the ties of her blouse.

"We really must go."

Gavin studied her. Lips swollen from his kisses, skin flushed and raven black hair loose from its pinnings, she presented the most enticing picture. At his regard, she began to fumble with her hair, loosening it and then braiding it quickly before pinning the tresses back up.

There was no prolonging their time alone. Gavin got to his feet and pulled Freya to stand. "What made ye so upset in the village?"

She closed her eyes as if pained. "I thought to have seen someone familiar, someone from my past." When she opened them, they were filled with something akin to desperation.

"Tell me the truth Freya. I cannae help ye otherwise," Gavin said taking her upper arm and guiding her toward the horse. "What do ye fear?"

Peering at the ground, she seemed dejected. "I am so sorry. I cannae trust anyone. I did in the past and because of it, I lost everything."

Her expression hardened and she lifted to look directly at

him. "Because of me my family is dead. Everything is gone. My home... everything." She whirled away crossing her arms.

Gavin wasn't sure what to think. A part of him knew she told the truth. However, by keeping secret who she was and where she came from made it hard believe everything she said.

"Those who killed yer family. Do ye think they search for ye?"

Freya shrugged. "I dinnae know."

Turning her to face him, Gavin tried to get more information. "Would it benefit them if ye were dead?"

Silence stretched until finally Freya shook her head but said nothing. Her shoulders slumped and the fiery woman he'd held in his arms, had made passionate love to seemed to disappear to be replaced with one who'd lost all hope.

"Freya tell me. Are they a threat to the clan?" It felt wrong to ask the question; however, his overall loyalty was to Clan Ross.

"He is a cruel man. But nae a threat to yer clan. It is only him."

When he reached for her, she tensed. It did not feel right to allow the conversation to overshadow what had occurred. He reached for her again and this time, she allowed it.

"I will do what I can to keep ye safe, Freya," Gavin reassured her, glad when she wrapped her arms around his waist. "Just come to me if ever ye feel threatened."

Freya let out a long sigh but said nothing.

The sun was setting as they made their way back. "I hope Flora has nae raised the alarm that we are missing." Gavin said looking toward the road.

"That is why I kept insisting that we leave." Freya sounded worried.

"I am sure we will come upon our guardsmen at any moment. I will explain ye felt ill and we had to stop until yer stomach settled." He pressed a kiss to the side of her neck. "Ye were very, very, ill, so it took much too long before we could continue forth."

When she shivered, he smiled against her ear.

As expected moments later a group of guardsmen, including Knox, appeared. Gavin gave them the explanation and by the worried glances toward Freya, they seemed to believe him.

Upon arriving at the keep, he helped Freya dismount. She insisted on going to her cottage alone, so he remained back with the men.

It didn't surprise him in the least when Knox gave him a pointed look. "Convincing explanation," his cousin quipped. "The others believed it." He motioned to the others with his head.

"What if she comes to be with child?" Knox asked.

Gavin pushed past him. "I am hungry." He headed inside to the great room and instructed the first servant he saw to ensure a meal was taken to Freya.

When Cynden approached, his brother's hazel gaze raked over him. "We didnae tell Mother ye were out alone. Are ye unharmed then?"

When Knox cleared his throat, Gavin didn't bother lying. "I rode back from the village with Freya, she was feeling unwell. We stopped by the creek and lingered."

"Ah," Cynden said. "I am glad nothing was amiss then."

"There were a pair of men on the road, which is why I went into the forest. I waited to reach the bend near where old MacTavish keeps his cows. Knowing they could nae see me, I rode into the trees and waited."

His brother and cousin exchanged looks.

"Did they continue toward the keep?" Knox asked.

"They never rode past the bend. Although they were a bit far, I could see them, and they were nae Clan Ross. It was just a pair of them, dinnae look like warriors. I could nae see any swords."

Something about the men had bothered him, they did not look familiar in the least. But at the same time, they didn't seem to be warriors as they'd not worn any kind of weapons. Looking past the others, he glanced toward the house. Was it possible they were who'd frightened Freya? Were they part of her past?

During last meal, he couldn't stop thinking about Freya. Several times, he missed what someone said as his mind kept wandering. He didn't need the distraction of a woman. Too much was at stake at the moment, and he needed a clear head.

Once he finished the meal, he went to find his mother. As expected, she sat with Ainslie. They'd finished eating and were in conversation, which stopped at his approach.

"Is something wrong son?" his mother asked, although she didn't seem at all worried.

"Nae. I have a favor to ask of ye both." He wasn't sure how to approach the situation, especially with so much unknown. At the same time, he couldn't allow Freya to continue to work as a servant.

"Can ye find another place for the woman Freya that's not the laundry. I am convinced she is highborn, and should her family come, it would be a slight if they found her working as a servant."

His mother motioned for him to sit, and Gavin lowered into a chair next to her.

"It is obvious that she comes from a background of privilege. While we traveled, I spoke to Alex about her. He does nae feel comfortable for her to be part of the household," his mother stated.

"And I dinnae feel she should be a servant." He did his best to keep his tone even, but his message was clear.

His mother nodded. "She can be Ainslie's companion if Cynden agrees. Alex may be against it upon his return."

Ainslie smiled. "I have no objections." She looked to where Cynden sat, and a silent message seemed to pass between them because his brother walked over.

Their mother spoke. "Gavin would like the lass, Freya, to be removed from her chores and be given a different role. I suggested that she become Ainslie's companion."

His brother's brow furrowed. "I dinnae see why her being in the laundry or with Ainslie makes much of a difference."

Cynden looked at his wife, his face softening.

Instantly Gavin wondered at the wisdom of putting Ainslie in danger. Although he believed Freya when she'd said not to think anyone would bring danger, he had the responsibility of assuring everyone's safety.

"Perhaps a different role," Gavin said.

"The lass requires shelter and our hospitality," his mother stated. "Now, go on yer way. Ainslie and I will speak with Freya and find a fit for her in the household."

Partly because they preferred not to argue with their mother and also because they had more important matters, Gavin and Cynden returned to where the warriors remained.

There was a crudely drawn map on the table and Knox gave assignments for each group of warriors. Every portion of the lands surrounding the border would be searched, even those by Munro's. Whoever the band of attackers were, they had to be along the border.

Once decisions were made as to who would ride where, Gavin went out. He told himself he wished to ensure his horse was fed and watered, but upon walking past Freya's cottage, he hesitated.

After a look over his shoulder to be sure no one saw him, he rapped on the door.

"It's me, Gavin."

Freya opened the door and moved back to allow him in. "Why are ye here?" She glanced past him. "Someone will see ye."

"I wanted to see ye and ensure all is well. How do ye feel?"

If possible, she was even more beautiful in the dim light of the single lantern in the tiny cottage.

"I am well. Ye dinnae have to see about me. I dinnae expect…"

He kissed her deeply fighting the urge to lift her into his arms and take her once again. Instead he stepped away. "I just want to ensure ye have calmed. Ye were upset."

Her gaze shifted away from his face and then back to look at him. Whatever she would say, he knew it was not entirely the truth. "I am well."

It was best not to linger, the last thing he wished was for there to be whispers about Freya. She was without protection and just the inkling that she allowed men into her home could bring unwanted attention.

"Come to me if ye need anything, if ye are in fear."

Freya placed both hands on his chest and peered up at him. In that moment, he wanted nothing more than to throw caution to the wind and remain with the beauty.

"I will. I assure ye." Her voice was devoid of emotion, but her eyes devoured him. She felt exactly the same way he did.

It was early morning the next day when Gavin and several men rode back to where he'd seen the strangers the day before. The morning haze had yet to dissipate, giving the hilly lands an eerie appearance. They didn't speak as they continued toward a wooded area.

Clan Ross guards had split into groups to patrol as much of the lands as possible. Each group had a pair of archers, who remained a short distance behind in case they were needed. The men required enough room to shoot their arrows.

Rustling from forest creatures scampering away was soon gone, leaving a silence only broken by the sounds of their horses and occasional birdsong.

"Someone has been here," one of the men whispered.

They continued on while searching the foliage and surroundings. Whoever had been there was gone. They could tell that by the fact no animals had been about when they'd arrived. Then again, it didn't mean anything as the creatures could have heard them approach.

Gavin considered that remaining in bed this morning would have been preferable to the chilly morning outdoors. The more time passed, the more he wondered if perhaps whoever the attackers were had gone.

Suddenly the unmistakable sound of horses cut through the silence. Whoever rode was in a hurry. Gavin held up his right hand, signaling for them to stop and listen. The closer the riders came, the more he wondered just how many there were.

Finally, through the trees, the riders were visible.

"Our men," Gavin said urging his horse forward. The riders hesitated upon seeing them, but only one slowed while the others continued on.

"What it is?" Gavin called out.

"The keep," the one who slowed replied. "Bìrlinns are headed there, they look like fighters and are nae slowing to announce their presence."

"We are about to be attacked," the warrior called out.

No other words were exchanged as Gavin and his men galloped to catch up with the others.

Things had just gone from bad to much worse.

CHAPTER NINE

WHAT HAD BEEN a quiet morning turned to chaos as news of a possible attack flew through the keep. Freya along with the other servants rushed to do as Lady Ross ordered. The moved tables to make room for those who'd come for refuge and waited keeping watch.

Soon it was evident that alarms had been sent out to the village and surrounding lands. Villagers and their families streamed through the gates. Within a pair of hours the courtyard was overspilling with people from the nearby farms.

ALONG WITH THE staff from the keep, Freya, Ainslie, and Lady Ross rushed to help those who required a place to settle. Already the great room was overburdened, mothers with young bairns finding a space on the floor where blankets were spread for them to settle for however long it took.

Guards kept the gates closed until people arrived. Several archers and other warriors stood atop the wall keeping watch. The rest of the Ross warriors were along the shoreline on the ground and others next to birlinns.

The unknown men in birlinns that had entered the sea inlet remained a short distance from the shore, not making it known what they wanted. From the way they'd not sent forward a messenger, it was obvious they were not friendly.

Although at a disadvantage being they would have to come closer to strike and would be within striking distance of the Ross archers, Freya prayed it meant they would turn around and leave.

She'd rushed to the upper story to peer out to the sea, noting there were three birlinns. Each with at least a dozen men.

Knowing she was needed to help, Freya went back down the stairs and through the great room passing crying bairns and worried mothers attempting to keep them calm. A pair of elderly people sat huddled next to the fire, their worried gazes following her progress.

In the kitchens, the scene was chaotic. Pots bubbled in the hearth, while maids chopped piles of potatoes and leeks.

Peigi, the red-faced cook kneaded dough, her hands working furiously as she barked out orders. "Wash the turnips and cut them into small pieces. Someone stir the pot."

A maid came up with an empty tray. "The bairns are hungry."

Peigi gave the maid a bland look. "The guards and Ross family will eat first. The rest can wait for the potato and leek soup."

Lady Ross walked in and spoke to a pair of lads. "Go and tell the stablemaster to slaughter a pair of pigs." The boys rushed out.

"I will pour ale and cider. It should hold off the young ones and elderly," Freya said, dipping a pitcher into a large vat of cider.

"For one day perhaps," Peigi insisted. "What if this goes on?" She looked to Lady Ross.

Before the woman could reply, a guard rushed into the

room, Ainslie on his heels.

"They attacked. Gavin insists ye and Lady Ainslie remain in the house upstairs." He looked to Freya. "Ye as well."

Freya's breath caught at being singled out. No one seemed to think anything of it, perhaps because of what occurred.

"Attacked?" Lady Ross and Ainslie asked in unison. "From the sea?"

"Aye," the guard replied and then attempted to usher them from the kitchens.

Lady Ross met the guard's gaze with an unwavering look. "I will remain in the house, but there is much to do. We will nae be cloistered in a room when the clan's people need us." She made shooing motions with her hand. "Go on to yer duties Miles."

After a hesitation, the guard finally left.

"Now," Lady Ross said looking to Ainslie and Freya. "Let us see about helping people get organized in the great room. We must ensure there is room for everyone to rest and sleep."

She turned to one of the maids. "When the lads return, have them dig a trench near the stables for when people need to relieve themselves."

Freya could see everything in a different perspective, what had seemed chaos earlier was not. Everyone had a responsibility and they moved about each other performing duties that were required.

As they made their way down the corridor, chambermaids hurried from the laundry with piles of blankets to make pallets for the people. They walked past a room that was normally the sitting area, the healer oversaw four younger men and women as they set up a room with cots for any injured.

Flora and Ainsley were soon setting up sleeping spots, ensuring everyone was given a small space and Freya rushed back and forth from the kitchens serving cider to the children and mothers.

The entire time her mind kept going to what occurred outside. Who were the attackers?

There had not been any flags on the birlinns. She knew it wasn't Tasgall, he didn't have any power or authority over a clan.

Where was Gavin? She'd not caught sight of him. She looked to the stairwell and considered going up to another level to look.

"Miss, can ye help me," an elderly woman had fallen on her side and Freya was pulled back into the fray of helping the distraught people.

FROM HIS VANTAGE point on the top of a hill near the shore, Gavin stood with the line of archers.

The attackers were Clan Mackenzie, there was no doubt in Gavin's mind. Why they'd chosen Clan Ross Keep was not clear.

With shields blocking the arrows, the encroachers managed to get their boats closer. Soon they'd be in water shallow enough to disembark, which would be the time for the Ross warriors to fight alongside the archers.

Unfortunately, it meant it would be harder for his archers to strike. The first of the Mackenzie warriors to disembark were soon cut down by the archers. His men loudly cheered each time a man fell.

Surely they had to recognize it was a suicidal mission.

"They must be desperate, to go to these lengths," Knox said lifting his bow, the expression on his face intent he loosed the arrow. A scream let them know he'd hit the target.

Gavin's stomach tightened as he concentrated. Pulling back on the taut string of his bow, he let out a breath and released. A man arched his back when his arrow plunged into it, then he fell face-first into the water.

Scanning the sea for more birlinns, he noted there were no other boats nearby. There were more of them, he was sure. If they'd split, it meant other Mackenzie invaders could be coming ashore near where his brother lived, or to the north, where they could approach by land.

Some of the invaders had reached the shore and were now battling with his warriors. It would be harder to hit them, so he concentrated on those making their way through the water. They were smart, crouched down with their shield blocking arrows, so he shot into the water hoping to hit legs.

The Mackenzie had not brought archers, at least not on the boats there. He turned and motioned for the young guard to come closer. "Take five men and ride along the shoreline toward the Macpherson lands. It could be some may have come ashore there. If ye do see them, do not engage. Warn the Macpherson and return here."

Once the guard left, Gavin continued his grim task. Below he noted Cynden in the fray and he hesitated. His brother's opponent was an excellent fighter.

Gavin lifted his bow and aimed at the duo, waiting for the right moment. Then it happened, Cynden stumbled backward, over a fallen man, and landed on his back.

By his opponent's stance, the man smelled victory. His younger brother would be angry at his interference. But Gavin would rather suffer Cynden's anger for his protection, than his mother's for not protecting him.

With a downswing of his sword, the Mackenzie warriors went for the kill, only to stumble sideways when Gavin's arrow sunk into his chest. Cynden had rolled, he would have avoided the strike. Just as the man fell dead to the ground, Cynden glared up in Gavin's direction.

"If nae for being occupied, he would attack ye right now," Knox murmured.

His cousin's gaze was locked forward, so Gavin didn't bother replying. Both knew full well that his mother would be bereft over the loss of any of her children. Cynden, however, was her youngest and if anything happened to him, she would become mad from the grief.

Few Mackenzies barely made it to land, most were struck down before they called a retreat. Ross warriors chased the bleeding and injured back into the waters, striking down those who were too slow to run.

Soon only one birlinns retreated back into the waters, Ross birlinns gave chase.

There was something wrong. Gavin sensed it through every inch of his body. Why would they send men to be slaughtered?

The last time the brutal Mackenzies had attacked, Clan Ross had perhaps thirty men in total in their guard, unlike now when they stood at over eighty. A lot had changed in the last two years, which the Mackenzies had obviously not been aware of.

"They were nae expecting us to fight back. Why else strike here?" Gavin said to Knox.

"A distraction?" Knox replied, thinking like Gavin that perhaps more came from land.

"To the other side of the keep!" They heard guard calling.

Thankfully Gavin and Cynden had thought ahead and had half of the men on horseback protecting the area surrounding the keep.

Upon nearing, they were met by the sounds of swords clashing and people screaming.

Gavin rushed into the keep and bounded up the uneven stone steps to the top of the wall, where he and several other archers joined the lines.

The Ross warriors were outnumbered, but not by much. Several of the attackers were archers, but they were useless once he and his men shot toward them. The Mackenzie archers were forced into hand-to-hand battle.

Gavin aimed and shot an attacker, the man gripped the arrow before falling from his steed. Half of the guard were still at sea battling the survivors, which meant they were now outnumbered on land.

At sea, there were more Ross than Mackenzie, hopefully word would reach them to retreat and come help.

The Mackenzie were smart to have attacked on both sides. It was unfortunate for them that the men who'd come by land had taken longer to arrive. Otherwise, it would have proven catastrophic for Clan Ross.

Commands were shouted and Ross Warriors retreated and lined up, then as one a line of men lowered long spears and charged forward.

The Mackenzies were not easy to defeat, their style of fighting aggressive and wild. It was as if they had no fear. Gavin notched an arrow, keeping watch for an opening. He recalled his father had told them once that the Mackenzies held Norse beliefs that they would go to a perfect place called Valhalla if they died in battle.

Soon the men were tiring on both sides. After he shot another Mackenzie, Gavin searched the fray for his brother. Cynden was holding his own. The muscled warrior had defeated his opponent and was standing over him.

Screams sounded as a woman, who's dress had been slashed open down the front, was dragged into the center of the fray. The fighting came to an abrupt stop, the Mackenzies retreated, and the Ross guards once again formed a straight line in front of the entrance to the keep.

Holding shields in front of themselves, two Mackenzie fighters held the poor lass by the arms, and one stood behind her. They shouted something Gavin couldn't quite hear.

The hapless young woman sobbed trying in vain to free herself.

Gavin narrowed his eyes, watching the interchange. "What are they demanding?"

"It could be they wish freedom to retreat," Knox said.

"Or want to enter," Gavin added. "Either way, they will kill her, the man behind her will cut her through."

There was little to be done, Cynden looked up to him in question. Gavin had no idea what could be done.

The lass cried out as one of the men who held her pushed the tip of his sword into her side just enough for blood to drip.

"We can give her a swift death."

"Dinnae make me do this," Knox murmured softly.

From below, his brother Cynden looked over his shoulder with the silent command. Knox inhaled sharply and Gavin pressed a hand on Knox's shoulder. "We can lose two arrows at once."

"What of the lass?"

"If I cannae get him, I will maim her. Be prepared." Gavin looked to the archer on his left. "Aim for one to her left."

"At one!" Gavin shouted.

The men who held the lass looked up.

The man to his left notched the arrow, aimed, and released. Hitting his target perfectly. Knox did the same and the men holding the lass fell backward, arrows in their chest.

Gavin aimed for the man behind the woman at the same time, hoping that the distraction of the others falling would give him an opening. Unfortunately, the man did not move.

Gavin released his arrow into the lass' leg, and she screamed and crumpled to the ground.

Another arrow hit the man who'd stood behind her and he fell to his knees and then face first atop the young woman who struggled to get him off.

There were shouts and the fighting began anew, this time the Ross warriors were relentless.

A Ross warrior rushed to the woman's aid, dragging her toward the keep where she disappeared from Gavin's sight.

Eyes sharp, Gavin continued to shoot arrow after arrow, ignoring the protests of his arms and shoulders.

The sun had fallen by the time the Mackenzie retreated and Ross warriors were able to get the last of the injured into the courtyard.

"THE BÌRLINNS OFFSHORE are gone. Probably to return on land if I were to guess," Cynden said as the sun fell.

Knox shook his head. "They have been planning this. I remember months ago when bìrlinns were spotted offshore. It must have been them."

No one spoke to Gavin. It was just as well, he couldn't see or hear anything other than the village girl's sobbing as she struggled against her captors And the look of shock and pain before slumping to the ground, an arrow protruding from her leg.

The pretty village girl called Gisela would have died without him injuring her. Despite knowing this, Gavin could not stop thinking that perhaps they should have waited to try and find another way. She could be hobbled for life.

IT WAS QUIET the next day, which meant the Mackenzies had gone into hiding. They would return, of that Gavin was sure. Already he'd sent a messenger to Uist to let Alexander know what occurred. He prayed his brother would be safe returning.

After the day of battling, his mother had taken to her bedchamber to pray. She'd not left since. Another reason to hate what happened.

The barbarians were not going to win.

Messengers had returned from neighboring clans stating they too had been attacked. Thankfully, most had held their own by combining forces.

With a contingency, Gavin patrolled the area near the keep, looking for any signs of the attackers. The air was thick with wariness, not only were they on the defense from the Mackenzies, but also from whoever had attacked their clan's people before their arrival.

There were shouts and two men on horseback neared his party.

The men looked from one face to another, with terrified expressions. One was younger with long dark hair, the other an older bearded man.

"We mean no harm. Dinnae have anything to do with whatever occurs. We seek refuge," the older man said.

Gavin scanned their faces. "Why are ye here? Ye are nae from our clan."

The same man held up both hands. "We were sent from Eigg to search for someone. Miss Freya Craig... her betrothed is worried about her. She was lost... at sea."

It felt as if someone had sunk their fist into his gut. He looked from the duo to his men, who kept a blank expression. "I dinnae know any Freya."

"She had black hair, is bonnie, with dark brown eyes," the man insisted. "There is a bounty... a reward for her return."

"I suggest ye leave Skye. We are at war at the moment. 'Tis nae safe. Ye can find refuge in the village, my men are along the road, ye should be safe. Go to the tavern, tell the barkeep Gavin Ross sends ye."

He motioned to the men, and they moved their horses so that the two could leave. The man gave him a questioning look but didn't say more before riding away.

"Did ye nae believe him?" one of his men asked as they continued riding toward the village.

Gavin shrugged hoping he came across as not caring. "I will have to ask the lass if it is true before handing her over to men we know nothing about. She is under our protection at the moment. I am nae going to allow strangers into the keep."

The entire time he rode, his fury grew. Why hadn't Freya told him she was betrothed?

If her betrothed was dangerous, he and his brothers should have the opportunity to ensure not only her safety but the family's as well.

The older man had been scared of what occurred. Gavin was sure what the old man had stated was true.

Anyone wealthy enough to offer a bounty could afford swords for hire.

Annoyed, he needed to tear his mind away from Freya and to the matter at hand. One threat at a time was how he'd have to handle things.

At the moment, the Mackenzies were the greater threat than a resentful betrothed man from another isle.

THE NEXT MORNING at dawn, the Mackenzies attacked again. This time they'd gathered united with the others who'd attacked other landowners on Skye.

They'd nearly doubled in size.

For half a century, they'd fought off the Mackenzies. The enemy clan claiming the land was their birthright. Whether it was true or not mattered little to Clan Ross. It was theirs now and it would not be handed over to idiots who attacked and killed their people.

Later that day. Gavin almost wept with relief when his brother, Alexander, returned from Uist.

He brought with him a large contingency of men sent by their cousin.

CHAPTER TEN

FREYA COULD BARELY function. Her feet, back, and arms were throbbing from constant work. Everyone in the household pulled their weight, sharing the tasks of cooking, serving, cleaning, and seeing after the injured. Lady Ross had disappeared into her chambers refusing to come out.

She'd been moved into the house at Ainslie's insistence as her cottage was required for one of the warrior's family.

Trudging up to her small bedchamber on the second floor, she hoped to lay down for a few hours before getting up to relieve someone else. Being up since dawn, Freya wondered how late it was. If she were to guess, it wouldn't be long before the sun rose.

When Freya woke, she felt rested and immediately bolted upright. Guilt assailed at the thought that she'd slept much too long.

To her astonishment, someone had refilled the large pitcher and basin in the room. As kind as the act was it felt much too indulgent. There were too many tasks on the shoulders of the household staff that they would take time to see after her needs.

Not wishing to linger overmuch, Freya removed her clothes and began washing away the dirt and sweat from the past couple of days. The water, although chilled, was refreshing. By the time she stood completely naked in front of the fireplace, Freya felt like a new person.

After a quick rap, the door began to open. Freya dashed sideways, grabbing a drying cloth to cover her nakedness. The fabric was not large enough to cover her completely, but she managed. Holding the cloth in place, she stared at Gavin, who hesitated at the doorway, then quickly closed the door behind.

"I should have waited for ye to reply." His green gaze roamed over her bare legs past the covering to meet her eyes. There wasn't any warmth in his expression, but more of a detached coolness when he looked at her.

"Did something happen?" Freya asked, not daring to move.

He studied her for just a bit longer. "Much is happening, as ye well know."

If he expected her to say something, it was lost on her.

"I am aware. I am helping where I can. As soon as I dress, I will go to the kitchens… or the sick room."

Once again his frigid gaze locked with hers. "During my patrol, I came upon two men. They are searching for someone. A woman with black hair and dark eyes. They are from the Isle of Eigg. They said she is called Freya Craig."

Her stomach dipped and throat closed, making it impossible to swallow. Her throat went dry, and she gasped for air barely able to get a breath. Her eyes watered and she fought not to cry.

Gavin didn't move. He watched her dispassionately.

"I dinnae know why anyone would come…" Freya began. The lie sounded weak even to her own ears.

"Dinnae lie to me," Gavin interrupted. "They searched for

ye. Called ye by name."

At her attempt to lie, the dispassion was replaced with fury. His lips twisted. "It seems yer betrothed is offering a reward for yer return."

She opened her mouth to say something, but Gavin interrupted. "As soon as it is safe, ye should go. It matters not if ye return to yer betrothed, it is nae my right to demand that of ye. But ye cannae remain here. If he is able to offer a reward for yer return, that means men will be coming to seek ye and it means danger for my family."

It was as if a vice gripped her so tight she could barely stay upright. Her legs threatened to give out, and her lungs refused to expand and retract.

"I must explain. There is so much ye are nae aware of." Her voice came out like a rasp.

Tasgall would force her into a marriage, he'd ensure her uncle would not be informed until it was too late. Then in all probability Freya would not live long. Once she was his wife the house, lands and family fortune would belong to Tasgall.

In a haze, Freya's eyes clouded, and she couldn't see past the tears. Terror gripped her at the realization that all was lost.

Freya's legs won the tug of war and she collapsed onto the floor, the cloth still gripped in her hands leaving her naked and vulnerable.

"Dinnae send me away. I beg of ye. I will leave. I just need time." Freya's soft sobs accentuated each word as she uttered them.

The cold floor seeped through her body, but she couldn't move. All she wished for at the moment was for Gavin to allow her the opportunity to explain. Even if he did, it was doubtful that he'd believe anything she uttered.

When he lifted her from the floor and carried her to the bed, hope sprung only to be dashed when he immediately retreated.

She looked up at him. "I should have told ye. It is that I am so scared."

Jaw clenched, it was as if he held back anger, or perhaps what she saw was a flicker of hurt. It was the worst possible timing for those men to appear. When his clan fought for their lives.

That he had little sympathy for her was expected. Yet she had to try. What she felt for Gavin was stronger than anything she'd ever experienced, and she believed he felt the same.

His eyes moved past her. "We will nae turn ye over to those men. But ye cannae remain here. Once it is safe…"

"I will leave," Freya interrupted him, internally pleading for him to meet her eyes and see the truth. To see that she loved him. "My betrothed is responsible for…"

"Stop!" Gavin shouted. "I dinnae want to hear it now. Whatever happened to ye before coming here, ye should have told me. I asked ye time and again."

With that he turned on his heel and stormed from the room. The slamming of the heavy door sent tremors through her.

She didn't cry. There were no tears left. This was another heartbreak to add to the many she'd already suffered.

To lose Gavin meant there was nothing more to hope for.

If it were not for the fact there was a battle ongoing, Freya would have packed and left. The exhaustion of the night before returned, but she slid from the bed and dressed.

As soon as possible, she would go to the village and find someone to take her to mainland Scotland. Perhaps she could find work at another keep.

The rain pelted her face the next morning when she opened the shutters to peer out. Gloomy and gray with heavy downfall, it was impossible to see far. It meant there would probably be no battle that day. Although she'd heard the Mackenzies seemed impervious to weather, it was doubtful they'd attack that day.

Since the laird had arrived with reinforcements, it had been quiet. Scouts must have reported it to the Mackenzies as they'd not reappeared.

Freya dressed in a hurry having decided that despite her having to leave, for the remaining time she was there, she'd continue to help the household. If not for someone having moved into the cottage, she would return there to make it easier to avoid Gavin.

The great room was a flurry of activity. Families who'd sought shelter were packing up, deciding to return to the village. The injured remained in the sitting room, being looked after. The usual long tables where people ate had been moved closer to the front of the room. There people huddled in groups having hushed conversations. Freya guessed they were deciding if it was safe to return home or wait.

She went to the sitting room to see about an injured warrior, who was alone. "Do ye require anything?"

He nodded. "Something to drink."

Freya went to a side table and poured ale into a cup then brought it to him.

Just then conversations ceased. The laird stalked in flanked by several men. He was one of the most striking men Freya had ever seen.

With raven dark hair and piercing deep green eyes, he was intimidating and stunning all at once. His shoulder-length hair flowed in waves just past his wide shoulders. Encased in a thick tunic, his muscular body was still evident. There was something about him that brought pause. Almost as if born for the role of leadership, he commanded attention.

Upon reaching the first bed, he stopped to talk to someone, then glanced to where she stood. Freya froze.

Was he about to come to her and ask that she leave?

To her horror, his eyes locked to hers as he walked closer and closer until stopping at the foot of the cot where the injured warrior lay.

He glanced at her. "Dinnae go. I wish to speak to ye."

Freya's blood turned cold, and she remained rooted to the spot.

"How do ye fare Xavier?" he asked the injured warrior.

"Well, Laird," the man replied with a grin. "Will be able to challenge ye to swordplay again."

The laird's eyes narrowed, but a smile played at the edges of his lips. "Challenge, aye. Beat me, never."

The injured man chuckled. "Give me a few days."

The exchange complete the laird returned his attention to Freya. He motioned for her to follow him outside past the great room and into the corridor that led to the kitchens.

Freya suddenly felt tiny when walking next to the huge man.

He hesitated just outside the great room his eyes scanned

over her, but not in a lusty manner. It seemed more curious than anything. "I am nae sure what occurred between ye and my brother. He is furious. I am informed men are seeking ye."

Swallowing past the fear, Freya nodded. "Aye. I was betrothed to a man called Tasgall Macgregor. My brother found out that he had our parents murdered. He wants our home and lands. That is why we escaped and ye know the rest."

His expression never changed. Was it something warriors perfected? To keep from others knowing their thoughts. "Why did ye nae tell us all this upon arriving? Why instead keep silent?"

"Because I didnae know if Clan Ross would send me back to them. I still dinnae know if ye and Laird Macdonald of Eigg are allies. The Macdonald and my betrothed's family are close."

Once again, the laird remained silent, seeming to be considering what to say to her. Finally he met her gaze. "Whatever yer reasons are, yer silence has caused more harm. My brother is…" He stopped midsentence and looked toward the great room.

"I will arrange ye safe travel to Uist. Ye can find work there at our cousin's keep in Uist if ye wish. He will be informed of the truth."

Freya nodded as trails of tears flowed down her face. "I didnae wish to cause harm to Gavin or anyone here."

Alexander's lips pressed together, and his eyes snapped to her. "Then ye should have been honest with him." The laird turned on his heel and walked back to the great room.

"Ah, there ye are." Una appeared from a doorway, carrying folded linens. "I was wondering if ye would be up. It was a long day yesterday." She continued talking and Freya walked beside her toward the kitchens. She was numb, unable to speak or think clearly.

"Go on in there and get ye something to eat. Then I need ye in the laundry," Una called out over her shoulder as she headed toward the door leading out to the courtyard.

Thankfully the kitchen was much too busy for anyone to pay her any mind. She ladled soup into a bowl and tore off a chunk of bread that she buttered. After placing both items on the tray, she walked back to the great room. She helped the injured man, Xavier, to sit up and placed the tray on his lap. "I will return to get it in a bit."

She repeated the action several times, with the other injured men in the room.

The day before she'd noticed they'd not been fed until late, so she wanted to ensure they ate well so they could recover faster.

It was much later that she finally broke her fast. Despite the hunger, the food tasted bland. How long before she left for Uist? After eating she would gather her meager belongings and move into Flora's room to allow someone to have the small bedchamber she'd been given. Staying in the servants' quarters would make it easier to avoid Gavin.

A part of her wanted to speak to him and try to explain. Perhaps the laird would tell him what she'd said.

Would it matter?

"Freya?" Una had reappeared. "Come along lass."

She stood and followed behind the harried woman, who showed her into the laundry. "Ensure to wash all the filthy blankets and clothes," Una said to her and the other two women in the room.

Just then a chambermaid walked in with another armload. "These are bloody," the young woman said, her nose wrinkled. "And they smell."

The task of stirring the laundry in boiling water with lye and then spreading it out to dry outside was laborious, but Freya was glad for the work. With it being so cloudy, it was doubtful the linens would dry, but at least they aired out as the rain, albeit much lighter, continued to fall.

When going back and forth to the well, she caught sight of men on horseback leaving the keep. She ventured once to the wall to look out. An archer approached.

"Ye should nae be here. It could be dangerous." He didn't seem angry, just spoke evenly.

"Those of us inside wish to know if any Mackenzies have been seen," Freya said.

The archer shook his head. "Not in the last two days. If ye ask me, they are gone to other places to attack."

"I pray it is so," Freya said. After another glance across the courtyard, she returned to her chores.

AFTER THEY FINISHED washing the linens, they began the task of washing clothes. Freya recognized a tunic, and she lifted it. It was Gavin's. She'd wanted to ask the archer if he knew where Gavin was but had been unable to form the words.

It was later that day that the rain finally ceased, and she went out to check on the clothes that had been hung earlier. Since it was quite windy, all were dry. She began pulling one after the other and folding them into a basket.

She hesitated and walked to where she could see across the

inlet. It was surprising to see several fishermen out on the water. People still had to eat and with only a few willing to fish, these men would most likely sell their entire catch.

On the shore a half sunken birlinn was the only indication of recent unrest.

Freya let out a long breath. There was no doubt that in the next day or two she would be gone. A part of her was thankful that the laird was willing to help her resettle. At the same time, how long before they came to look for her no matter where she went.

Perhaps it was best she leave on her own. Not tell anyone where she headed. It would be safer for the people of Clan Ross.

CHAPTER ELEVEN

Gavin was glad the rain had been replaced by a brisk wind. His clothes were finally dry enough that he and his men were a bit more comfortable as they continued riding along the shoreline. So far it had been another fruitless day of searching for the damn Mackenzies. No birlinns had been sighted leaving, which meant they'd either remained hidden, or had somehow managed to escape on land.

"Unless they can fly, they must be here somewhere," Knox said while scanning the surroundings. "There are too many of them to hide in one place."

At last count it was at least fifty men who'd survived the last attack.

"Why Skye?" Gavin asked no one in particular. "I can understand the upper Hebrides, or northern Scotland."

Knox shrugged. "They thought it would be easy. Probably still think this land should be theirs. We are nae heavily populated and until recently had no real guard to defend us."

"I suppose in a way, the Mackinnon did us some good," Gavin replied ruefully. Referring to the fact that after fighting the MacKinnons, they'd recruited men from Uist to join the guard force on Skye.

A picture of Freya's despondent expression formed, and he closed his eyes. She'd looked so pitiful lying on the floor naked and sobbing. He never wished to see her like that again.

He'd been unable to leave her there and had lifted her to the bed. The urge to cradle her and soothe the woman until she stopped crying had been so strong that he'd almost climbed into the bed.

Somehow, he'd managed to keep a distance, the only way to maintain perspective. She was betrothed. Belonged to another and had not told him.

Whatever her reasons for leaving, that she'd not been honest was what mattered most. He suspected it was not a match she'd desired and had somehow convinced her brother to take her away. Although her explanation made sense, Freya's leaving her home had caused her brother's death.

A part of him wanted to return to her and ask for a full explanation, but he knew it was best to stay away. Her presence could potentially bring his clan more conflict. It was the last thing they needed.

Knox rode up alongside. "Scouts return." Both watched as two riders came closer. By their lack of expression, they'd not found anything of use.

"News?" Gavin asked dispassionately.

"Nothing. No one has seen anything," one of the horsemen replied. "As if the earth swallowed them."

The second scout motioned past him with his head. "A shepherd was attacked by a group of men. He survived long enough to tell his family the men who attacked him were MacKinnons."

Gavin wanted to scream in frustration. Instead, he dismounted and walked toward the shoreline.

What was happening? They were fighting two enemies and

were not close to catching either. As frustrating as it was, he knew they had to concentrate on the bigger threat.

Both scouts rode off toward the Keep Ross, to inform Alexander of the latest news.

"We will nae find anyone along the shoreline," Gavin said watching as his men emerged from a group of cottages finding them empty. Most of the people who lived there had sought the safety of the keep.

Knox rode to him. "Let us go in the direction the scouts came from. If it was the same men who attacked, they've become bolder and are more inland."

It was a short while before they came to a heavily forested area. They slowed to allow Knox to take lead and search for any sign of travelers. When he motioned them forward they continued into the trees.

Six men would not make themselves known to a contingency of warriors, but at the same time it was best not to take chances.

The wind whistled through the branches as they continued in silence, the only sounds were the rustling of branches as the horses rode past.

Then suddenly a soft whistle was heard, followed by several arrows whooshing past. One Ross warrior fell from his horse, the rest immediately lifted their shields. A couple of Ross men had arrows protruding from their bodies but remained upright.

At first it was hard to tell where they came from until Gavin saw several men in the trees.

He was surrounded by shielded men as he set an arrow in the bow, pulled back, and released through a small opening.

A direct hit from the sound of the man yelling then falling to his death.

They'd only three archers against however many there were in the trees.

The arrows continued to rain down. On the ground they were at a disadvantage. At the same time, now that they knew where the Mackenzies were it would be easier to flush them out.

Once past the tree line and out of the archer's range, they would keep watch to ensure the men would not leave the area without being seen. A scout was dispatched to the keep. Those wounded, if capable, were also dispatched back to the keep. That left only ten warriors including Gavin.

"Go with them," Knox said with a worried look. "Go back to the keep."

At first Gavin didn't understand. "Ye speak nonsense. We are outnumbered until more warriors come."

When Knox looked to his side, he followed his cousin's line of sight to where an arrow protruded from the left side of his torso. In response to the awareness, it was then that trails of pain seared through him, and Gavin gasped.

"If ye would have stayed quiet," he groused flinching at the throbs of pain.

"I doubt I can ride back," he admitted. "Help me down, I can still shoot."

With a worried expression, his cousin took hold of the reins of Gavin's horse and pulled him to the side of a hill.

His breathing was becoming labored, each breath bringing stabs of pain. He groaned and attempted to take more shallow breaths.

Gavin swung his leg over the saddle and allowed Knox to help him from the horse. Then he lowered to the ground, doing his best not to jostle the arrow. If he guessed correctly, it was almost all the way through. However, pushing it out could bring blood loss and he couldn't afford it at the moment.

"Break off the end so that it does nae stick out so far."

Without hesitation, Knox bent and broke the arrow. Gavin held back a cry at the pain, not wanting to expand his body and cause more damage.

"We best prepare, they will come after us as soon as they climb down from the trees," Knox said walking toward the other men.

There were only nine Ross men left without him. If Gavin were to guess, there had to be almost double in the trees.

Pain or no pain, he had to help. Peering up to the top of the hill, he decided it would be an advantage to be higher.

"Knox!" he called out and his cousin turned. "Tell the other archers to come. We will fight from atop the hill."

Two archers ran over, slung their quivers and bows over their shoulders, then taking Gavin under the arms as he clutched his items, they dragged him up to the top of the hill.

Pain shot through his body, and Gavin cursed under his breath. "I do wish to be alive to help."

The men gave him apologetic looks. He understood. It was best to be prepared because the men in the forest were well aware of their current advantage in numbers. However, the Mackenzie men didn't have horses.

Understanding reinforcements would soon arrive, men emerged from the forest, shields up rushing at the Ross warriors.

It was hard to aim because the men moved constantly while fighting. Gavin and the other two archers didn't want to take the chance and strike a horse or one of their men by mistake.

The Mackenzies fought savagely. When a horse fell from a strike to his leg, Gavin pulled back his arrow intent on killing the man. Thankfully, his arrow struck true, and the man collapsed next to the fallen horse.

The Ross men were at a disadvantage when one was felled. The two archers dropped their bows and quivers, unsheathed their swords and raced to help.

Although outnumbered, the Ross warriors held their own fighting back-to-back. Gavin concentrated on the battle, ignoring the pain. He pulled arrows and shot when he had a clear view. It was becoming harder to keep his strength up.

Choosing a particularly large man who carelessly lowered his shield as he sliced across the air with a huge sword, Gavin pulled back the string, holding it taunt waiting for the precise moment.

The man roared and charged toward one of the archers, praying the archer did not move to the right, Gavin loosed the arrow. It struck straight into the larger man's chest, and he looked down in shock.

Instead of collapsing, he continued charging. Gavin loosed a second arrow, this one striking the left side of the man's chest. The man hesitated for a moment, then took another step before falling forward.

The numbers were equalizing, and the Mackenzies seemed to realize it because they called retreat.

They came to their lands. Attacked their people. The Ross

warriors would not let them escape.

With each pull of the bow's string, his body protested. Gavin tightened his muscles in an attempt to keep his trembling body steady enough to aim.

Just then a Ross warrior collapsed, his opponent rushed toward him, sword lifted. he managed to pull the string back one more time.

Gavin took a deep breath and shot. The arrow struck the man in the lower portion of his chest, and he stumbled backward. It was enough of a distraction for another Ross warrior to cut him down.

His vision blurred as he notched another arrow. Blinking fast, he tried to focus on another fighter. Swaying slightly, Gavin's arms trembled. It would be dangerous to try again, but he would not give up, not until every single one of the attackers fell.

He took a shallow breath, pain searing down his side and once again tried to concentrate on the battle below. His legs went out from beneath him, and the arrow flew up into the sky as he toppled sideways.

"GAVIN." A DEEP voice pulled him from a dark haze. But it proved impossible to respond. There was no pain, just a comfortable abyss and he didn't have any desire to leave.

"Do ye hear me?" the same voice asked, and he wanted to tell whoever it was to be quiet. The darkness seemed to pull him deeper, and he welcomed it.

Gavin wasn't sure how much time passed until the same

deep voice spoke again. It was close now, as if in his mind. "Brother. Ye must wake."

Brother? The word was familiar. The voice as well. But it didn't make sense. The only thing he wanted was to remain in the darkness and not emerge. Ever.

Jostling was startling. "Wake up," the same deep voice insisted.

This time, he recognized it. "Alex?" He tried to say it aloud, but his voice was like air.

"Gavin," the voice said. "Open yer eyes."

The darkness seemed to evaporate. Little by little until it remained like a fog on the edges. Gavin opened his eyes and was immediately doused by brightness. He covered his face with both hands.

"Close the shutters," his mother ordered and instantly the room dimmed so that opening his eyes became bearable.

"Is everyone well?" he asked in a hoarse voice. "Knox?"

"He is alive and well. Was injured, but recovered quicker than ye," Alexander said, looming over him. "Ye gave us quite a scare," he scolded as if it was Gavin's fault.

His mother grabbed his hand. "I am so glad ye awakened." His mother's face was taut with worry. "It has been days."

A cup of ale was brought, and his brother helped him to drink. He drank greedily. "How many days?"

"Three," Alex replied.

"The Mackenzies?"

"The ones who survived the last battle left in boats."

"The damsel awakens," Cynden said strolling in with his usual scowl.

Gavin narrowed his eyes at his younger brother. "What are

ye doing here. Should ye nae be getting yer hair braided."

The comment made Alex and his mother chuckle. "I think he will be fine," his mother said stroking his hair and then kissing his brow. "My sweet lad."

The healer walked in with Freya right behind him carrying a pot of water and cloths. "I must see to his wound."

Freya kept her gaze down, not noticing Alex's icy regard. His brother was obviously not pleased to see her, but he kept silent.

"I must see to yer wound," the healer stated.

Everyone but his mother left the room.

CHAPTER TWELVE

Somehow Freya managed not to gasp at walking in and finding that Gavin had awakened. He had a pillow beneath his head and shoulders, so he wasn't flat on his back, but not quite sitting up. Still his gaze locked on her as soon as she walked in. Freya had looked away, concentrating on what she carried, fully aware the laird would not be happy to find her there.

Although fully expecting that she'd be sent away, it had been Gavin's injury that had kept the family distracted from doing so. Not only that, but every warrior was busy patrolling the Ross lands. Once finding areas safe, they began escorting those who'd sought harbor in the keep, back to their homes.

Several families, who lived in the furthermost farms were still at the keep waiting to be escorted back. It was a time-consuming process. Freya was astonished at how well the laird cared for his people. Not one person's safety was ignored. Even the surly ones, who demanded to be next.

Gavin's bedchamber was dim.

"Can we open the shutters?" the healer asked. "I must see."

Freya waited for Lady Ross to nod, and she put the pot of hot water and clean clothes down and opened the shutters. Sunlight poured in and she noticed Gavin closed his eyes and then blinked them open while adjusting to the brightness. He met her gaze and for a moment they looked at one another.

Freya looked away first and hurried to stand next to the healer.

The blanket was pushed down past Gavin's stomach. The bandage wrapped around his midsection had a dark bloody stain, but it was dry.

"We will have to pull ye up to sit. It may hurt, but I dinnae expect it to be too bad," the healer said to Gavin and grabbed his right hand.

"Take his other arm," he instructed Freya sliding his hand under his arm.

"Slowly," he said as they pulled Gavin up to sit.

Gavin moaned and let out a harsh breath his face contorting. "It-it h-hurts pretty badly," he gritted out.

"The arrow went through, and the injury was made worse by what I imagine is ye continuing to fight. It tore through a great deal of flesh."

Lady Ross made a strangled sound and Freya glanced to her. "Do ye need to sit down my lady?"

The woman had become pale. "I hate to see my lad in pain." She gave Gavin an apologetic look, tears glistening.

"Mother, please go."

Lady Ross seemed about to argue, but Gavin repeated the request, and she went from the room.

"Now, we must unwrap the bandage, do ye think ye will be able to remain upright?" the healer asked, and Gavin nodded.

It was then Freya realized she was still holding his arm. She pulled away without looking at him.

As the healer unwrapped the bandage, he asked Freya to wet the area with a wet cloth so not to tear away at his wound.

She moved from the front of him to the back as the healer removed the wrapping. It felt almost intimate to be so close to him. To touch his body. Thoughts of being with them in the forest formed and were hard to push away.

Finally the bandage was removed to reveal a jagged cut that had been stitched closed.

Gavin looked down examining it. "How is the back?" He met her gaze as he asked.

Freya leaned down to look at the back wound. "Not as large. About half the size."

Once the healer cleaned the wound and slabbed a thick poultice to the area, they wrapped a new bandage around him.

"I will instruct the cook what to make for ye. 'Tis important ye eat as much as ye can."

The healer looked to the bloody bandages and crimson water. "Ensure to clear it all out."

Freya nodded and picked up the pot, then proceeded to pour the bloodstained water out the window. She then stuffed the dirty cloths into the same pot to take down to the laundry.

"Can ye fold a blanket behind my back?" Gavin asked. When Freya looked up, she noted the healer had left them alone.

"Of course." She hurried to do as he asked. When he didn't lean back, she waited. "Do ye need help?"

Gavin let out a breath. "I know it will hurt. Cannae be worse than what I have already felt."

"I will help ye." She went to stand beside the bed and held him by the shoulders. "Slowly."

He grimaced, letting out soft grunts.

This was perhaps the only opportunity to speak to him in

private and Freya would not let it pass. She went to stand at the foot of the bed.

"I owe ye an apology," she began.

Gavin's gaze bore into hers. It felt like a caress, and she fought not to touch him again.

Finally he spoke. "There is nothing to say Freya."

"I should have trusted ye," Freya continued not willing to let the moment pass without her saying something. "It is just that I was so very afraid. He killed my parents."

He nodded but remained silent. The fact he didn't react meant that in all probability he didn't believe her.

"First my father, then my mother. Beathan, my brother, found out. He overheard two men talking about how they would kill him next. They planned to ask him to go hunting and then return with stories of how he'd died. That is when we escaped. We dinnae have time to get anything…" The words stopped when grief choked her, making it impossible to keep talking.

"If that is true, then the fact ye both arrived in such horrible shape makes it believable. What will ye do now?"

His tone was flat. If he'd ever cared for her even a bit, it was gone. Trust had been lost and he would never allow her close again. Every emotion crushed through her. Despondency the strongest.

"Yer brother has offered to send me to Uist."

Finally he looked at her again. "I wish ye well."

It was as if someone had sliced through her and Freya flinched, her breath escaping in an audible whoosh. She grabbed the edge of the blankets and pulled them up to cover his wounded midsection.

His hand covered hers, and when she looked at his face, his eyes were closed.

She leaned forward and pressed a kiss to his lips. "I am so very sorry. The one thing I am grateful for in all of this is to have known ye. I should have trusted ye with my secrets." Freya grabbed the tray with dirty bandages and fled from the room stopping just a few feet in the corridor as sobs overtook and she crumpled to the floor.

"Freya." Flora hurried by with a tray. "Stay there, I will return shortly."

Her friend went into Gavin's room. It was not much later that she emerged without the tray. "He insists he can feed himself. Quite surly, which means he is definitely recovering," Flora chatted, lowering to sit next to her.

Many times, Freya had been thankful for her friend, now more than ever. Flora didn't expect explanations but accepted things as they were. And if Freya shared then Flora listened.

"I am going away," Freya finally said, her voice just above a whisper. "The laird is sending me to Uist, to his cousin, Laird Ross' household."

"To keep ye safe?" Flora asked. When Freya gave her a questioning look, her friend smiled softly. "It is obvious by ye nae speaking of yer past, that ye are running from something. Or someone."

Freya nodded. "Aye, to keep the people who killed my family from finding me. And they dinnae wish for my presence to bring more chaos to this clan."

"I dinnae want ye to go," Flora said, her pretty face etched with sadness. "Ye are my first good friend."

"I dinnae wish to leave ye either," Freya replied. "But I

must go. There is no other recourse."

Flora looked toward Gavin's door. "What about him?"

Obviously not much had gotten past Flora. "He does nae trust me because I never told him why I was here. He is rather angry with me."

"That is selfish," Flora said crossing her arms. "Ye were only protecting yerself. If it was nae that I am but a servant, I would tell him myself."

Freya couldn't help but chuckle. "Ye are a good friend."

THAT EVENING FREYA was still in the chamber on the second floor. Una had insisted another girl had to stay in Flora's room and that Freya had to remain in the one the family had given her.

She paced and thought about the fact she'd leave shortly. Perhaps she could try speaking to the laird again and ask to remain at the village. Not that it would do any good. She couldn't guarantee that the Tasgall wouldn't send a larger group of men after her. Although they'd be no match for Ross warriors, it didn't mean it was a welcome probability.

There was very little to be done, but to pack her few belongings and prepare to leave.

Unable to sleep, she grabbed a shawl and left her room. There was a light coming from a doorway and she walked closer. It was Lady Ross' sitting room. Freya would ask to sit with her for a bit, but upon voices spilling out, she stopped.

"Ye should allow her to remain," Lady Ross said. "I think it will help Gavin."

"What of her past?" It was Alexander, the laird who spoke with his mother. And they were talking about her.

"Do ye trust her, Mother?"

There was a beat of silence before Lady Ross replied, "What is there nae to trust. Send someone to find out. We have friends in Eigg, why not send someone to find out what occurs there? If it is true that the Craigs were slain, then perhaps those responsible should be brought to justice."

Alexander cleared his throat. "Why would I go to all this trouble? I have other more important matters. We have nae found out who is behind the attacks prior to the Mackenzies coming."

"For yer brother. Once Gavin is better, if ye wish to send her away do it then."

The silence continued for longer and Freya decided it was best she return to her bedchamber.

Lady Ross was concerned for Gavin, which was understandable. Still it hurt to hear that they would simply "send her away" at Gavin recovering. Her presence wouldn't help anything. If she'd mattered to him in the slightest, it was gone now.

Most of her belongings were already packed. Freya grabbed the last few items and tossed them into a sack. Then she crept down the stairs and went to the servant's quarters.

She pushed the door to Flora's tiny room open, placed her bundle on the floor and then climbed into Flora's bed. The lass stretched and yawned, sleeping cap askew, she could barely keep her eyes open.

"I've decided to leave. I will go today," Freya whispered.

Flora scrunched her face. "Explain why ye are leaving on

yer own."

"I must. Tis best no one knows where I go. I do wish for ye to inform the laird once they discover I am gone. I dinnae want them thinking the men who search for me had something to do with it."

"What will I say?" Flora asked.

"Tell them that I decided to leave on my own. That I preferred no one know where I go."

Flora looked on the verge of tears. "Will ye nae tell even me?"

Freya's own eyes stung. "I plan to find a way to get to mainland Scotland. Perhaps find employment there. I am nae sure how to go about it, but hopefully something will occur to me."

"That is so very dangerous," Flora exclaimed. "So much can go wrong."

"I know." Flora wiped away an errant tear. "However, I never planned to remain this long to begin with. Tis best I go."

BY THE TIME the sun rose, Freya was at the village. She'd been fortunate that a man with a cart was heading to Tokavaig after bringing items to the keep. The older man was friendly and seemed thankful for her company as he chatted the entire way, not bothering to ask her any questions about exactly where she was headed. He accepted her initial explanation of being a servant going to visit family.

Once in the village, she walked to the stables and inquired about going to the mainland. The stablemaster was an intimidating man, who eyed her with barely concealed distrust. "I have never seen ye before. Where are ye from?"

Freya gave him her best innocent look. "I have been working at the Ross keep for months now. I rarely leave. Now I must go visit my ailing grandmother."

"Wait here," he replied and walked away in the direction of the tavern.

When he returned, another man came with him. Freya pushed away her fear and met the men's gazes.

The man seemed nice, of medium build, older. "I leave to Dornie, I can take ye that far."

Hope instantly sprung. "When do ye leave?"

"Today." It was all the man said and the stablemaster chuckled.

"Martina is taking her time packing then?" The stablemaster asked.

Freya perked up at hearing a woman would be traveling. "I can help her. I have nae else to do but wait."

The man's house was a long walk, by the time they got there, a red-faced woman greeted her husband with narrowed eyes. "And where have ye been? I have been loading everything on my own." She ignored Freya and continued glaring at her husband. "At the tavern, eh? Had to see yer lads before leaving, I bet."

Finally she seemed to notice Freya. "And ye, where did he find ye?"

"The stables… I am offering to pay to go along with ye," Freya answered.

"Come on then, put that in the back." The woman pointed at her sack. "Norman, fetch the last of the things while I have a bit to eat." She looked Freya over and then gave a little nod. "I bet ye 'ave nae eaten."

Freya followed a surprisingly swift Martina into the house, where she rushed to the hearth and began frying eggs and waving a cloth around to shoo chickens out the back door. "Eat before we leave or the chickens will steal it," she called out.

A young man walked in, he eyed Freya for a moment then stood next to the door with a bored look.

"See after the chickens. Ensure to feed them. Do nae burn the house down son," Martina instructed between bites.

The chaos of Norman and Martina's household was a welcome distraction from her heartbreak.

It wasn't much later that they rode away from the village at a slow pace. Martina spoke nonstop about visiting her family and how she'd come from there with Norman to Tokavaig when newly married. She grumbled about missing her family and how she'd been trying to convince Norman to move there.

"Is there a large estate nearby that perhaps I can find work?" Freya asked.

Martina eyed her. "I suppose if ye worked for the Ross, ye can work at the castle there. Clan Macrae may welcome the help. Nae too many villagers live nearby,"

Freya eyed the sky, it was heading toward the afternoon. Had her absence been noted yet?

If so, no doubt the stablemaster would inform whoever came asking. She'd not thought and had been honest about where she worked.

When Norman and Martina stopped to rest for what seemed like the tenth time, she wanted to scream in frustration.

"How much longer before we arrive?" she asked, following

Martina to some bushes. "I must find a place to sleep once there."

"We should arrive before night fall. Ye can stay with us until morning," Martina replied.

"I dinnae wish to be a bother. I can stay on the back of the wagon." Freya peered toward where they came from looking for any signs of riders.

Martina chuckled. "Ye will nae do anything of the sort."

Upon returning to the wagon, Norman stood looking to the distance where two men on horseback ambled in their direction.

Freya's blood ran cold at the sight. Praying it wasn't the duo from Eigg, she narrowed her eyes attempting to see them clearer, but they were still too far away.

Norman motioned for them to hurry to the wagon. "Come now. Dinnae want to catch their attention." It was evident he meant Freya as his gaze landed on her. Freya's breath caught and she nodded as she and Martina clambered onto the back of the wagon.

She pulled a cap from her bag and stuffed her hair into it, then pulled it low. Martina gave her a quizzical look but didn't say anything. Thankfully she'd thought to carry the dirk Gavin had gifted her in the pocket of her skirts.

Sitting in the back of the wagon meant she couldn't see the men, so she settled down and pulled her knees up to her chest calling on all the holy beings that they continue on without stopping.

It seemed only moments later that the riders called out to Norman. Norman exchanged words of greeting.

The men continued past the wagon. Freya held her breath,

not daring to look up. Just as they passed one of them hesitated.

The horses came to a stop.

Freya's blood ran cold, she kept her face turned.

"Freya." Tasgall's voice was level.

She finally looked up and was met with his cold gaze.

He looked to Norman, who'd climbed down and stood between the horsemen and the wagon.

"What happens?" He looked to Freya. "Do ye know this man?"

Tasgall's bark of laughter sounded hollow. "Aye she knows me."

Norman seemed at a loss at what to do.

"Do nae interfere," Martina pleaded softly.

Freya's voice shook and she spoke in a whisper so only the woman could hear her. "He is dangerous. Go with yer husband. I will leave with him, I do nae wish to put ye and yer husband in harm's way."

Tasgall and his companion pulled swords and Norman took a wobbly step backward. The older man was no match for them.

"Leave them be. I will go with ye," Freya said scrabbling from the back of the wagon.

Tasgall dismounted and walked to Norman holding the sword to the man's neck. "They can alert whoever ye were staying with."

"They do nae know anything," Freya insisted, pushing herself in front of Norman.

The slap was so hard, she fell sideways. She'd not seen him raise his hand until it was too late.

Martina cried out at seeing Freya fall, but her eyes went back to her husband, who kept his ground.

"Let them go," Freya scrambled to her feet and rushed to Tasgall, who kept his sword at Norman's neck, seeming to enjoy the discomfort he was causing the older man.

He grabbed Freya's hair, pushing her toward the horse. "keep your mouth shut."

Slicing across, he cut the older man's upper arm. Norman and Martina both cried out. The man stumbled backward in shock.

The cut didn't look deep, at least that's what Freya hoped.

Tasgall glared at the older couple. "Donnae follow us." He turned and went to where Freya stood.

Norman managed to climb onto the bench and with his wife's help they urged the horse to take them away.

The further they went, the harder Freya shook. Her only hope now was that someone would come looking for her. They had to traverse through Ross lands to get to the shore where they would catch a bìrlinn headed for Eigg.

Tasgall grabbed her by the shoulders his face transformed into a mask of fury, upper lip curling and nostrils flaring. "Because of ye, I have had to leave my duties to search ye out. I am nae pleased with ye."

"Ye could have declared me dead. I am sure ye and yer family are already living in my home. Claiming my lands."

This time his fist sunk into her stomach, and she fell to the ground as all air left her body. The strike fanned the embers of hatred that already existed. Freya could barely move, her legs almost gave out when he yanked her up to stand.

"I feel sorry for ye Tasgall. That yer greed has pushed ye to do things there is no forgiveness for." Her words rasped out, barely above a whisper.

He lifted his hand to strike again, but his companion spoke up. "Enough Tasgall, we must find a place to sleep. Cannae have her all bruised up. People will notice."

His hand wrapped around her arm so hard she flinched. Yanking her to the horse he lifted her upon it then mounted.

It was best to keep a clear mind. Freya hung her head as if in defeat not wishing to alert him that she was considering when to kill him.

CHAPTER THIRTEEN

Gavin pushed himself from the bed. He held his breath expecting throngs of pain, but thankfully, it wasn't as bad as he'd expected. There was tightness making it hard to take deep breaths, but other than that, he could move without the urge to moan.

He'd lost too many days. Thankfully the threat of the Mackenzies was gone, as far as they knew they'd left after realizing how big of a mistake it had been to attack Clan Ross. They should have sent scouts, or perhaps they'd done so and had been misinformed. Either way, they'd lost a lot of men in the effort to take over Clan Ross lands.

Knox had informed him that their guards had gone out to hunt any that remained behind. So far only two had been found. One in the woods, hiding in bushes and on the verge of death. He'd died within moments of being found. The second one had sought harbor at a farm, where a woman had been caring for the feverish and delirious man. They'd left him to either recover or die as the woman had defended him, bravely holding up a small dirk. "it would be a sin to kill a man already on his deathbed," she'd scolded.

He went to the window. A group of mounted men were heading out for their daily patrols. There was still the matter of the Mackinnon men who'd they'd been searching for. The men had proved to be wily. There were many places to hide, the simplest one was probably among the villagers as they'd not be given up by their own families.

Gavin lifted his arms miming the movements of pulling back the string on a bow. His injured side flared, and he lowered them. It was too soon.

The door opened and Flora entered with a tray of food. She looked to him with a wary expression. "Should ye be standing? Ye could fall."

Shrugging he slowly lowered onto a chair. "I am nae one to lay about."

The maid placed the tray on a table next to the chair. "Ye look better."

"Has Freya gone?" He wanted to pull back the words that he'd not dared to ask his brothers. Alex had told him the warriors from Uist would be leaving that day or the next.

"She has gone." Flora's brow furrowed, but she pressed her lips together, unwilling to say more, but she didn't make to leave either.

"Ye wish to say something?" Gavin urged.

The maid seemed to consider her words. "She cares deeply for ye, sir. It was fear that kept her from telling ye everything."

In his estimation, he'd reassured Freya, and she should have believed him. "Without trust, there is nothing."

"How hard would it be for ye to trust if someone killed yer family?" Flora gasped lifting both hands to cover her mouth at realizing she'd spoken too freely. "I apologize." The maid ran from the room.

The food lost its appeal. He stood up, albeit slowly, and returned to the window. Nothing seemed amiss, the portion of the courtyard he could see was no longer filled with people. Instead, several men stood talking, he recognized them as guards. Other than that, it seemed all had returned to normal. Whatever that meant.

He took several steps toward the doorway, ensuring to take slow breaths and not exert himself. Once at the doorway, Gavin continued to the stairwell.

When stepping down with his right leg all was fine; however, the left was another story. The action made his side stretch, which was painful. And he'd never realized just how many steps there were to reach the great room.

By the time he stood on the landing, he was out of breath and sweaty. His brothers, Cynden, Munro, and Alex sat with Knox and a pair of warriors. Everyone stopped talking and looked to him.

"What are ye doing?" It was Alex, of course, who would chastise him. "Ye should nae have come down unassisted."

He ignored his eldest brother and went to the table where he lowered gingerly to sit. "Ale please."

A tankard was placed before him, and he drank it down greedily.

There was an awkward silence, and clearing of throats as those seated waited to see what Alexander would do about Gavin.

"Why are ye here?" Gavin asked Munro.

His brother looked to Alex who replied. "Another attack. This time to one of Munro's men."

The laird let out a breath. "Continue Munro,"

"As I was saying," Munro said eyeing Gavin. "When he didn't show up for practice, a pair of my men went to search for him."

Gavin gawked at his brother. "Why did no one tell me there's been another attack?"

"Because we are just now finding out," Cynden said giving him a pointed look. "Ye should be in bed."

"I am nae that badly injured." Gavin looked around the room, expecting to see Freya although knowing she'd gone.

Knox spoke next. "Did anyone see the attack?"

Munro nodded. "Some bairns were playing in the woods. They saw the group come upon him. They said he fought back, but there were six of them and easily overtook him."

"Aren't yer guard all MacKinnons?" Gavin asked.

"Aye, most. He was nae. It was Seamus."

At his brother uttering the name, Gavin squeezed his eyes shut. Seamus was young. Had only joined the guard force a pair of years earlier. He'd been Munro's squire before then and had followed him when he'd taken over for the Mackinnon.

"He was returning from visiting family in the village here," Munro added, his face twisting with rage. "He didnae have a chance against six."

"Cowards," Alex growled out the word. "We must find them and make them pay for this."

They continued making plans to begin scouring for the attackers.

"We will begin with the village near me," Munro said. "We got good descriptions from the bairns. One of my men admitted to one of them sounding familiar by what the bairns described."

Knox grunted. "If not in the village, I venture to guess they must be hiding near or on yer lands Munro. They know that area much better than the ones closer to this keep."

As they discussed, a pair of maids entered and began scrubbing tables. Another walked in with a tray piled with bread and different cheeses.

Movements brisk, she came closer and waited for Alexander to notice her. When he did, she asked if he wished for the food. His brother motioned to a nearby table. "Put it there, we can fetch it if we desire."

As much as he wanted to ask about Freya, he wouldn't do it in front of the others. As they continued to talk, he returned his attention to the subject at hand, his mind reeling. How was it that these men had gotten away with the attacks for so long?

Each man got orders as how to proceed from Alexander and left to relay them to their men.

Alexander gave Gavin a pointed look. "Go back upstairs and rest." He walked from the room toward the doorway.

Knox remained back, leaned back in the chair, his keen gaze taking Gavin in. "Ye will nae be able to ride for at least a sennight."

"I am aware. I can still help with…" Gavin couldn't quite think of what he could do other than perhaps hear villager's complaints."

His cousin chuckled. "I am nae one to lay about either, but needs must."

"Freya?"

There was a stretch of silence as Knox considered the question.

His gut twisted. "Tis not a hard question to answer. What happened?"

"She left." Knox let out a breath. "Tis for the best, I suppose."

"To Uist?"

Lips pressed tight; Knox shook his head. "Nay, she left on her own."

Air left his lungs, and he searched his cousin's face. "What do ye mean? Where to?"

"We can never hope to understand women and how they think. She dinnae leave any message. Just went on her own. May not have wished to go to Uist."

"Did anyone go after her?" His mind was reeling. How could they have let her go and not ensured she'd not come to harm?

Knox didn't have to reply. Nothing had been done. There were more pressing matters with the recent Mackenzie invasion, his injury and other guards still recovering. Then there was the matter of the six men attacking clan's people randomly.

"There were people looking for her. The ones she was running from." He didn't mention the attackers could have gotten her. The thought of that made him sick to his stomach.

"What can we do? She is free to do as she wishes."

Gavin glared at Knox. "How long since she left?"

When his cousin shrugged Gavin wanted to hit him. "Not sure. One of the maids Flora told us the day the warriors from Uist were returning. I would say two days, perhaps three."

Ignoring the pain, Gavin stood. "I will send someone to find out where she went." He wasn't foolish enough to try and mount, at the same time, it was hard to trust that anyone would care enough to search for her as diligently as he would.

Knox held up a hand to stop him from walking away. "I've already made some inquiries," he admitted hesitating before continuing. "She went with a couple that were headed to Dornie, the small village on the mainland. She is safe."

"Ye did that?" Gavin wanted to kiss his cousin.

"I knew ye would be… er upset when finding out she'd gone. Gavin, ye must let her go. The lass never planned to stay here. As ye said, people are looking for her and the last thing we need is more trouble for our people."

He tried to remember the last words he'd said to her. Gavin let out a breath.

A sensation of foreboding overtook him, and he met Knox's gaze. "Other than the attacks, has anything else happened?"

"Nay," Knox replied seeming relieved he'd changed the subject.

"What of the Clan Mackenzie?"

"A few stragglers here and there. We have a pair here who gave themselves up. Alexander has yet to decide what to do with them. Keeping them locked up in one of the rooms for now."

They didn't have a dungeon, which meant prisoners were usually kept under lock and key with guards outside the door.

"Are ye patrolling today?"

Knox gave him a knowing look. "Aye, I and three are assisting in patrolling near Munro's lands. I will make inquiries about Freya."

Gavin let out a breath and nodded.

The hardest part of the healing process was going to be the inability to help in the search for the attackers. Not only that, if he were to be honest, he would have already ridden out to search for Freya to ensure no harm came to her.

Whether he was ready to admit it or not. He was in love with her.

CHAPTER FOURTEEN

Tasgall had a bìrlinn waiting when they arrived at the shore. Freya had hoped to get a message to Gavin somehow, but it had been late in the day, almost night when they'd finally made their way onboard. Not one soul was about in the hidden cove where the boat was docked.

Once on Eigg, there was a wagon waiting as well as two horses and they'd made their way to her family home.

She'd rebuffed any attempt by Tasgall to get her to talk, liking the angry sparks of annoyance in the glares he directed at her.

Once at the house, she'd been ushered to a guest room. She knew the reason for not giving her one of the family rooms. It was Tasgall's way of showing her he was now in charge. Little did he know she preferred the anonymity of the guest room, not wanting the reminders of a life lost.

She'd slept fretfully, refusing to open the door when someone knocked. It wasn't until late the following morning that pangs of hunger finally led her to leave the room and head to the kitchen.

One of the servants, a woman called Edina hurried to her, when she entered. "We were told ye and Bethan were lost at sea." The woman's hands shook when they reached up and cupped Freya's face. "Thanks be to God ye are back."

Words couldn't form as Freya's throat was blocked with emotion. Memories of times of Edina and her mother spending their afternoon cooking or discussing over tea came flooding back.

Freya hugged the woman, who began to cry softly. "I was so afraid for ye. None of us knew what to do."

"I survived. Beathan did nae." Freya closed her eyes refusing to cry. "There is much to talk about, but…" She stopped at hearing footsteps, placing a finger over her lips to let Edina know not to ask her to continue.

"Awe ye are here. Tonight, I am hosting a celebration of yer return," Tasgall announced as he entered into the room.

Neither Freya nor Edina spoke.

Tasgall regarded her for a long moment, and she met his gaze refusing to cower. It was satisfying when he looked away first. The curl of distaste on his upper lip did not go unnoticed. One way or another, he planned to punish her for the insolence.

He turned to Edina. "Prepare a menu. My mother will review it with ye."

Edina looked to Freya.

In two strides, Tasgall closed the distance and shoved Freya aside. He stood directly in front of Edina. The woman's wide eyes looked to her feet. "See mother for any questions ye may have. Is that clear?"

The woman's head bobbed up and down. "Yes Sir."

"Come." Tasgall took Freya by the arm, his fingers digging cruelly into the skin. She tried to tug it free, but then cried out when he tightened the hold even more.

They went up the stairs and into the largest bedchamber, which had been her parents. Their belongings were gone, every surface was bare. The bedding had been changed. By the tunic tossed over a chair, Tasgall slept there now.

"Once we marry and share a bedchamber, I prefer it be the largest one."

If he planned to do anything, Freya vowed to fight with all her strength. Once she'd thought to love him, had thought him the most irresistible man. Now she was repelled to even consider that he'd been her lover.

When she yanked her arm away, he released it. "I care not if ye donnae wish to lay with me. Once or twice will be enough, at least until ye give me an heir. After… I can get my needs met elsewhere. It was never… very pleasurable with ye."

Now that she'd been with Gavin, Freya realized never to have enjoyed joining with Tasgall. It had always been quick, ending abruptly. Thankfully he'd ensured not to crest explaining that his father would not forgive a bastard child.

With Gavin, it had been the most beautiful experience, not a duty she'd been cajoled into by her betrothed.

Freya went to the window and peered out. It was best not to allow him to know what her thoughts were. She'd yet to come up with a way to get away from him.

"I will nae marry ye." Freya turned to look at him. "Ye cannae force me. I know what ye did. Ye had my parents killed. If nae for us leaving, Beathan would have been next."

He shrugged and closed the distance. "And yet he did. Die that is."

Before she could think, she slapped him hard across the face.

Tasgall's hands wrapped around her throat, his eyes bulging in fury. "Ye little bitch."

Clawing at his fingers didn't help the lack of air and Freya fought to breath. Then just as quickly, he released her.

Gasping in lungsful of air, Freya coughed with the effort blinking away stars that formed behind her eyelids.

Grabbing her chin, he forced her up to meet his narrowed eyes. "Be sure to dress formally for tonight."

TASGALL AND HIS parents stood near the entrance later that day as the guests arrived. Meanwhile, Freya kept an eye on who arrived from the second-floor landing, keeping just out of sight.

There were people she didn't remember ever meeting, and four couples who'd been friendly with her parents. She wondered what had been said to them, or if they were more loyal to whoever they thought had control of the wealth that came with the house and lands.

Tasgall kept looking around the room and to the stairwell expecting her to stand at his side and greet the guests with a united front.

Never would she stand beside him again.

She waited until everyone was seated and a second maid was sent to find her before she finally went down to the great room.

It must have been both her expression and lack of a proper dress because at her entrance, conversations stopped, and the atmosphere turned tense.

From the awkwardness of those that knew her parents, it was obvious they'd been told stories about the reason for her absence. If Freya were to guess, Tasgall had said she'd gone mad with grief and traveled away to have time alone. Or something of that matter.

That some of the guests had called themselves friends to her family, had been close to her mother and her father, and now they shared a meal with their killer made her stomach clench.

It was possible they didn't know the whole truth, but surely everyone had to suspect she and Beathan would never have left without a good reason.

Tasgall stood and held out the chair next to him so she could sit. Freya didn't give him so much as a glance. She went to the chair and lowered, the entire time considering what to do to ensure everyone was aware things were not what they seemed.

"I am sure everyone is glad to see Freya has returned," Tasgall said in an overly jovial tone, lifting his glass as if to toast.

When Freya kept her hands folded in her lap, not touching the glass in front of her, the guests seemed unsure of what to do. Only a pair reached for their cups.

"Let us lift our glasses in welcome," the oblivious Tasgall instructed, with a wide grin. "My betrothed has returned." He'd acted as if she'd been on some sort of holiday, instead of running for her life.

Finally everyone, except for her, lifted their cups.

Tasgall turned to her. "Freya?"

She scanned the faces of those around the table and stood. "What are we here to celebrate? That my parents were murdered? Or that now my brother Beathan is also dead."

There were gasps accompanied by everyone looking to one another with confusion.

Freya couldn't keep the sneer from her lips. "How dare ye gather and toast as if all is well. Have any of ye even bothered to find out if what Tasgall says is true? That Beathan and I went away willingly?"

At the smell of food, her stomach revolted, and Freya threw up, the contents of her stomach spewing across hers and Tasgall's place settings. If not for the tightening of her stomach muscles threatening a repeat performance, Freya would have laughed at Tasgall's shocked expression.

There was a moment of silence followed by some people making retching sounds.

Tasgall's mother covered her mouth, her face turning a sickly green. She pushed back from the table with such force that the chair toppled backward. Gathering her skirts with her free hand, the woman rushed out of the room. Those closest to Freya pushed away from the table as well.

Taking a cloth, Freya wiped her mouth. She swayed on to her feet. Doing her best to ignore her stomach's tightening, warning that it may react again. By now almost everyone was standing, moving away from the smell.

There were no feelings of embarrassment or any feelings at all, truth be told. Instead, she looked around the room meeting each set of eyes.

"This is my family home. It is nae *his* home." She pointed at Tasgall, her hand shaking slightly.

Then she motioned toward the doorway. "None of ye are ever welcome here again. Leave my home at once."

No one moved, instead they looked to Tasgall, who gave

her a murderous look. "Ye are nae feeling well. Nae yerself, darling."

"Ye odious pig. Ye had my parents killed. And ye are responsible for Beathan's death. How dare ye sit here and play host? I wish for ye and yer family to leave my home at once. Everyone get out!"

"Ye must calm. Dinnae forget that we are to marry…" Tasgall said through clenched teeth.

"I will never marry ye!" Freya's voice was like a screech.

Whirling to the people who watched them with rapt attention, she lost all control. "I said get out! All of ye, get out!"

Spurned by her screams, the guests finally reacted and one by one, hurried from the room. Soon they were all gone, except for Tasgall and his father who stood by the doorway, he looked to Tasgall as if wondering what had caused the night to go so wrong.

Tasgall's father had always been a quiet unassuming man. At the same time, he was imposing, and Freya knew that beneath the seemingly calm exterior was an iron rod will.

She'd like Tasgall's parents but didn't trust them now. Still she could not be positive the man was not involved, so she refused to give him any benefit of the doubt.

"Ye should nae make those kinds of accusations in public," Tasgall's father told her in a gentle voice. "There is no proof of it. I am sure ye are mistaken, lass."

Tasgall stood by the sideboard, glaring at her. She'd ruined his moment; his attempt to prove to the local affluential families that in fact he did hold clout. Freya almost smiled.

She shook her head returning her attention to the older man. "Beathan overheard Tasgall speaking to several men, planning to kill him."

Tasgall tensed, his gaze turning hard. "He lied to ye."

Freya ignored him keeping her gaze on the older man. The man seemed willing to hear what she had to say. Still she didn't totally trust him.

"According to my brother, Tasgall just as admitted having my parents killed when told the men Beathan had to be next. That's what he said, "next," she said emphasizing the word.

Tasgall's father looked to his son, searching his face. "Go on," he said to Freya.

"Why else would we leave? We had to escape, in an attempt to save my brother. Now he is dead. Succumbed to lack of food and water." She hated the pitch on the last word.

The older man's eyes widened and moved from her to Tasgall, who watched her through slitted eyes. He was furious and no doubt plotting how to turn things around in his favor.

Before his father could speak, Tasgall said. "Ye are nae making any sense. Yer parents died in an unfortunate manner, they were struck down by robbers. I had nothing to do with it,"

Then he looked to his father. "There is nae proof I had anything to do with their death. I was with ye and Mother at the time."

Freya let out a huff when noticing a tightening of his right cheek, something he did whenever he lied. His father must have noticed it as well because his eyes narrowed.

"We will leave yer home," the older man said without inflection. "Once things calm, the betrothal will be discussed because it was a formal agreement made between yer father and myself."

"We are betrothed. Our betrothal was a formal and witnessed agreement forged by our fathers," Tasgall repeated, once again. He closed the distance between them, trying to intimidate her. Freya refused to show fear, keeping her feet firmly planted.

Again her stomach churned in warning, and she let out a sound of warning.

Tasgall hesitated when his father spoke. "The lass has been through a great deal. We should give her a few days to rest and think clearly."

"We will go." His mother appeared in the doorway. She'd still not regained her color as she met Freya's gaze. By the stricken expression, she'd overheard it all. There was pity, or perhaps an apology in the way the older woman regarded Freya. "I wish to leave at once."

Acknowledging he'd not make any headway that day, Tasgall let out a hard breath. "Fine. But I will return in a few days, along with the cleric and constable. At that time we will formalize everything."

Whatever that meant, Freya didn't like it. Tasgall's family was wealthy, especially now that she suspected he'd dipped into her father's coffers. She'd yet to search for where her father stored his gold and other valuables, not wanting to be spied on by Tasgall and his family.

It seemed to take forever before they left and when they finally closed the door behind them, the house plunged into silence, even the candles seemed to dim as she collapsed into the closest chair.

Edina, who'd been in the family's service since she was a child hurried into the room. "Drink this," she said shoving a cup into Freya's hands. "It will settle yer stomach."

Freya drank the overly sweetened hot liquid and let out a long sigh.

"What am I going to do Edina?"

The woman lowered to the chair next to hers. "Whatever ye decide, we will help ye," she said referring to herself and her husband Colin.

From Tasgall's warning, she only had a few days to come up with a way to keep him from the family wealth. Whether she ended up impoverished didn't matter, what was important was to ensure a murderer did not end up with control of her home and lands.

She could go to the village priest and seek council. Of course if the man didn't believe her, it could possibly do more harm than good. After all in the end it was her word against Tasgall's, especially as Beathan couldn't testify about what he'd heard. There was also the impediment that the betrothal had been formal, with witnesses that had included the priest.

AFTER DRESSING THE following morning, Freya hurried to the front room to find Edina. The woman's face brightened upon seeing her.

"Ye were brave last night, miss."

"I need yer help," Freya said, not feeling brave at all. She was too anxious that at any moment Tasgall would return with a constable and a clergy who would force her to marry him.

"Edina, fetch Colin at once," she said referring to the woman's husband. "I need him to deliver a message for me. Please hurry."

When Edina left, she began pacing a nervous energy filling

her. It was late the night before that she'd come up with an idea and a way to keep the home and lands out of Tasgall's hands. But she'd have to act quickly.

The only person who could help was her uncle, her father's brother William.

He was married and had a son and a daughter. As her father's male relative, and Freya not married, he would be the one who would inherit the land. Not that he would ever demand it.

However, once she explained to him what had occurred, Her uncle William would advise if her plan to give him the home was a way to keep Tasgall from ever seizing it.

With both her father and brother dead and she the only living member of the family, surely he'd understand that she had the right to do what she wished with the property.

It meant it would no longer be her home, but at least Tasgall would never own it. Her heart quickened and she prayed her family would agree to come at once.

Edina's husband came through the door. Colin was a kind, softspoken man. Slightly stooped, thin and he walked with a slight limp, his plain face brightened at seeing her.

"Miss Craig. So glad to see ye," he said.

"I am glad to see ye as well," Freya replied, genuinely meaning it. "I have an important task for ye. I will pay ye extra because it is imperative ye leave immediately."

"No need for that lass. I will go at once," Colin said, his head bobbing up and down.

She proceeded to give him specific directions to her uncle's home, which was over half a day's ride away.

"Inform him I have very good news for him and that the

entire family must come at once. Ensure he understands that time is of the essence. Tell him, he is saving my life by coming."

Edina and Colin exchanged concerned looks, but neither seemed surprised at her words. When Freya held out a tartan pin that belonged to her father, the older man took it.

"Give it to him to prove that ye are indeed sent by me in case he does nae remember ye."

CHAPTER FIFTEEN

GAVIN'S SIDE ACHED, but he managed to ride along with Knox and Hendry. They followed a path along the edge of the forest, keeping an eye out for other riders. It had been several hours of riding, it was past midday and his stomach growled with hunger.

"We can seek a meal at the village," he said to his companions. "Ask questions to see if anyone has seen the men."

It didn't take much encouragement, Knox had been discreetly directing glances toward him to make certain he was not in too much pain.

It wasn't much longer that they arrived at a small establishment in Armandale, the village on Munro's lands. The eatery was run by two elderly sisters. Once seated, they were presented with hearty bowls of stew and chunks of bread to eat with it.

One of the women eyed Gavin up and down. "Are ye kin to the new laird?"

"I am," Gavin replied between bites. "He is my brother."

"Ye seem to be hurting." She walked to another room and returned with a cup of steaming liquid. "I put some herbs in here to help with the pain."

He eyed it suspiciously, so she lifted it to her lips and sipped. "Tis nae poison."

Gavin studied the woman, noting there was warmth in her eyes. "We seek six mounted men, who have attacked several defenseless people. Do ye know of band of men riding about?"

The woman shook her head. "People come in, we serve them." It was clear she was not going to give them any information.

"What of strangers? Men ye have never seen before? Anything of note lately?"

She hesitated. "A few days back, a couple stopped by to ask for help. The man's arm was cut through. He bled badly. They were traveling west to Dornie, when a pair of men came and took a young lass that traveled with them. The woman, Martina, said they would have killed her husband if not for the lass stepping between them."

Gavin's mouth went dry. It had to be Freya who'd been taken.

"The men… were they from here?"

The older woman shook her head. "Nae."

"How do ye know?" Gavin was becoming exasperated.

Knox placed his hand on Gavin's shoulder. "When did this happen?" He asked.

Looking from Gavin, the older woman replied. "Less than a sennight, five days, perhaps six."

"Did they say the lass' name?" Gavin asked fighting to keep his voice even.

The woman shrugged. "They'd only just met her. Said she had hair dark as midnight. She was a sad little creature, looking for a new start."

"Did they overhear where they were taking her?" Gavin asked, ignoring Knox's pointed look.

"Aye mentioned something about returning to Eigg," the woman replied turning away.

Despite the blood roaring in his head, Gavin finished eating, all the while considering what happened to Freya. She must have been trying to get further away and instead had been caught by the very people she hid from. If she'd remained on Skye, she would be on Uist now, safe from the man who pursued her.

"It could be she ran from a husband or hid from her father. We have no way of knowing the truth," Knox remarked, obviously reading his thoughts. "Going to Eigg will only serve to delay yer recovery."

"She is in danger. Without family, she is at the mercy of whomever took her."

Knox was silent and Gavin was glad for it. He had thinking to do. Despite the fact she'd kept things from him, he could not deny that he wished she were still on Skye, at his home. If only he'd insisted she remain. Instead he'd allowed anger and rashness to take control and now she was in all probably held captive, perhaps being mistreated.

If harm came to her, it would be his fault for not standing up for her, for not helping or giving her the opportunity to explain things.

"We should continue our search while the sun is up," Gavin said after finishing the meal.

They mounted once again and headed out of the village in the direction of Edgar's cottage. In his gut, Gavin sensed that the men who'd attacked were either hiding or gone to another portion of Ross lands. It was possible as well that they'd left the isle to bide their time.

Once again his mind went to Freya.

"It is a bad idea," Knox said without looking at him. "Ye are nae fully healed and to go to another isle without knowing what awaits is a fool's errand. Ye have no idea what happens there."

Gavin ground his back teeth. "Stop doing that."

A bark of laughter erupted as Knox threw his head back. "Yer thoughts are clearly visible."

Both looked to Hendry who stared at Gavin and then shook his head. "I am nae able to see it."

"That is because ye are nae a Ross," Knox told him. "We can read each other's minds quite well."

Gavin rolled his eyes. "Dinnae believe him Hendry."

They continued on for a pair of hours. Gavin's side throbbed and he finally had to ask that they return to the keep.

"That was a waste of a day," Hendry said with a long sigh. "No one admits to seeing them. It is an impossible task."

"Aye," Knox added. "They cannae hide forever, sooner or later someone will talk."

"Since the last attack, they've kept away. It's also possible they've not returned to our lands."

Deep in thought they continued their trek back to the keep. Gavin was already planning to travel to the Isle of Eigg. He had to see with his own eyes that Freya was alive and well. Else, he'd not be able to rest.

ONCE AT THE keep, he went to Alexander's bedchamber. That his brother was there was odd. His eldest brother usually spent the days dealing with the many clan issues at hand and rarely retired until late in the evening.

The room was large with an imposing four-poster bed centered along the wall directly in front of the door. A large rug covered the stone flooring, upon it a pair of chairs. Alexander sat in one, his gaze on the fire that burned brightly in the hearth. He didn't seem tired or upset, if anything, Alex's expression was one of calmness. The laird glanced up when Gavin entered.

"How do ye feel?"

Rounding a chair, Gavin went to the other one, which was closer to the fire. "I must admit to having to returned from patrol early because my wound ached. However, if pushed, I am able to do almost as much as before."

After a moment, Gavin added. "Why are ye here alone? Is something wrong?"

Alex shook his head. "Nae, nothing that matters. When I noted no one waited to speak to me, I came up here and am contemplating what to do about our problem at hand…" Alex looked to Gavin. "Before Da died, things were different. Now all I do is worried, plan, fight."

"Ye have a heavy yoke, brother." Gavin's statement hung in the air.

Finally Alex nodded. "Strange that before I always had a hobby or interests to occupy my free time. Now, as laird, I am much too busy for anything that interests me."

"Ye have never been one for idle time. It is both a gift and a curse."

It was good that Alex was in a pensive mood. Still, Gavin wasn't sure how to bring up Freya. At the same time, it was imperative that he did so.

Finally, he took a breath. "I wish… I am going to the Isle of

Eigg." He continued not allowing Alex time to formulate a response. "I found out that a pair of men took Freya from the back of a wagon when she headed to Dornie with villagers from Tokavaig. I cannae allow her to possibly be in a harmful situation and nae do anything about it."

For a long moment Alex studied him. "It is much too dangerous, and with the attackers about, I cannae spare any men at the moment to go with ye."

He wasn't about to be dissuaded. "The attackers have gone into hiding. Even if they come out and continue to prey on our clan, we cannae capture them unless someone comes forth and tells us where they hide."

Alex shook his head and let out a grunt. "We should be able to protect our people from this. Somehow these bastards have managed to evade us. Someone, or perhaps a group of people are helping them."

By his brother's grim expression, there was something else afoot. Gavin leaned forward. "Is there something else on yer mind?"

As the silence stretched, Gavin allowed it, waiting for Alex to speak. Finally his brother took a deep breath.

"During our trip to Uist, Mother brought up that it is time for me to marry. One of the questions Darach asked, was why I had nae sought a wife as yet." His brother's deep green eyes lifted to his, a furrow between his brows. "In all honestly, I'd not given it much thought. Each time I consider it, my stomach clenches in dread." He visibly shuddered. "I do nae wish to be tied down to one woman."

Gavin chuckled. "By yer reaction, I'd say ye are nae ready. Ye would make the poor lass miserable."

Alex let out a huff. "Marriage is a restriction."

"Then wait. I dinnae see what the hurry is," Gavin said.

"And yet, ye are willing to go into the unknown to find a lass ye barely know," Alex remarked. "Interesting."

"I didnae say I was to marry her," Gavin protested. "It is just that I feel responsible—"

"One step away," Alex interrupted. "Ye are in love and will marry the lass. That is if she is nae already wed."

When Gavin stood, his injured side protested. After a day of riding, he required rest.

His brother stood as well and gave him a pointed look. "I know ye well enough to understand ye will go with or without my permission. Take five of our best warriors. Dinnae take any risks. Find out what ye can before approaching."

"I will." Gavin walked out, not wishing to speak more on the subject. First thing in the morning, he'd leave for the Isle of Eigg. Rest would have to wait, there was much to do.

First he'd find five men willing to go, then the bìrlinn had to be stocked to ensure they could remain self-sufficient for at least a fortnight. Then he needed to pack personal items. He hurried down the stairs and straight outside suddenly barely feeling the pain. He continue through the courtyard, not stopping until arriving at the guard's quarters.

Once there, he found Hendry and asked the warrior to find four more who were willing to travel to another isle.

Next he sought out the storehouse man, who was instructed to prepare provisions for both he and five men. Lastly, he spoke to the stablemaster to ensure the horses would be ready first thing in the morning to embark on the bìrlinn.

Once all that was completed, he went to the great room to wait. The men would eat last meal with him where he would explain the situation. His plan was to find Freya and make sure she is unharmed. Other than that, Gavin didn't dare plan for anything else.

Upon entering the great room, he scanned the room until finding his mother already seated at a small table where she, Cynden's wife, Ainslie and another pair of ladies usually ate. She was alone at the moment.

"Mother, I am to go on a short trip in the morning. Only two or three days at the most. To the Isle of Eigg."

Concern etched her face as she took him in. "The lass, Freya."

Somehow everyone seemed to know how he felt. It was as if he was the last to know. "Aye. I wish to ensure she is unharmed."

"Ye must be with care, my darling. Promise ye will be safe."

Gavin nodded meeting her gaze. "Mother, Alex is nae ready to marry. Ye should nae pressure him."

"He will have to, and the sooner the better." His mother waved him off as a pair of women approached, signaling the conversation was over.

It could be his mother already had a lass in mind. It was possible. If so, Alex didn't have a fighting chance.

During last meal, Knox informed Gavin that he'd not be going to Eigg. It was not surprising, his cousin led a large contingency of Ross guards and had to see to things there at the keep.

THE SUN WAS barely past the horizon the next morning as Gavin and his men were already on the bìrlinn headed toward whatever awaited them on the Isle of Eigg.

CHAPTER SIXTEEN

"No one is coming," Freya told Edina as both stood outside looking in the direction of her uncles' lands.

Edina gave her a hopeful look, her lips curving just a bit. "I am sure they will come. It takes time to prepare a family for travel. Yer uncle has nae been here since yer parent's funeral."

"If only Beathan and I could have gone to them instead of out to sea. But we were terrified of being caught by Tasgall and his men."

Edina took her hand. "Come let us walk for a bit. Ye must be tired of being cloistered in the house."

They strolled down a path that led around the back of the house. Freya studied the lands and then looked back to the home. As familiar as it was, something vital was gone. It was as if the spirit of the home had been taken from everything. The garden her mother had planted remained and her father's favorite cane rested next to a chair in the sitting room. And yet, they would never return to touch either.

Freya linked her arm through Edina's as they walked. "I have to admit that I do not mind giving it all to my uncle. Without my parents and Beathan, it no longer feels like home to me."

Edina's look of astonishment made Freya pause. "But it is yer home, miss. Ye were born here. Yer father had this house built for yer mother, he expected to raise ye and yer brother here and for ye to do the same. I am sure he meant for his descendants continue living on these lands."

"I am the only one left and cannae own it because I am a woman. Whomever I marry would lawfully own the house and lands. I have no desire to allow someone, especially that monster, Tasgall, to have it all."

"I understand." Edina sighed.

They continued walking, rounding to the side of the house when in the distance men on horseback appeared.

"Go inside, miss. They are too far for us to see who they are," Edina said moving with surprising speed, she more pushed than guided Freya to the front of the house. Then she called out to two men who worked in garden and stables to come. "Do not allow them inside the house until I see who it is."

Edina and Freya went inside and hurried up the stairs into one of the bedchambers and looked out through a large window.

It took a few moments before Freya's heart sank. It was Tasgall and his ever-present companion.

"At least he doesn't bring the clergy or constable with him," Freya told Edina. "I will meet with him outside. I prefer he not enter the house. Instruct men to remain close." They went back downstairs.

By the time Tasgall and his companion neared, Freya stood atop the steps in front of the house, the two workers on the ground on both sides.

Tasgall peered down at them before dismounting. He took inventory of the surroundings, his gaze pausing on the two men who kept their gazes on him.

"I've come to see if ye have calmed down enough to be sensible." His gaze was dispassionate when taking her in. "Our wedding ceremony will occur as soon as I get the clergy and constable to come. Ye can prepare or nae. But it will happen."

Freya hitched her chin. "As I said before, I will never marry ye."

Stalking toward her, he ignored the two men and went up the stairs to stand over her. Freya motioned to the two men to remain where they stood.

All he had to do was reach over and push her off the steps. She'd be hurt if she fell from this height. Still she maintained her ground waiting to hear what he had to say.

"Ye have no choice. Our betrothal was made public. The agreement made between our families was formalized. Ye cannae do better for a husband."

If not for him seeming on the brink of losing his temper, Freya would have laughed. She glanced toward the road, mentally willing her uncle to appear. But it was empty, not a person in sight.

At her silence and lack of reaction, his nostrils flared, and lips pressed into a tight line. "Three days hence ye will present yerself for marriage."

Freya took a step back forcing a bored expression. "Ye are willing to spend every night for the rest of yer life with one eye open wondering which night I will kill ye in yer sleep? Seems a steep price for a house and lands. The inability to trust a wife who wishes ye were dead."

Tasgall's eyes widened, but then he quickly regained his composure. "I could threaten ye the same."

The blood in her veins turned ice-cold. If she was forced to marry, it would be a race to see who would kill the other first.

Interesting.

She felt no fear, just a strange calmness.

Something in her demeanor must have changed because Tasgall studied her with curiosity. He turned to look at the men, who watched him with ill-concealed hatred. "Although yer father was an adequate manager, I can make these lands prosper."

"Ye are a fool."

Tasgall lifted his hand to strike her.

"I wouldnae do it," a deep voice sounded, and everyone turned to see a man dismounting.

It was her uncle.

Freya let out a long breath of relief.

Tasgall went down the stairs his demeaner deceivably calm. "Ye must remind me who ye are. I know we have met before."

William Craig was tall and broad. At least a head taller than Tasgall. And although older, he was an imposing man. Despite this, Freya feared what Tasgall would do. He was always armed with daggers.

Her uncle ignored Tasgall and looked up to Freya. "How are ye lass?"

"And ye are?" Tasgall repeated with impatience. "This is a private matter at the moment, perhaps ye can return another time." He motioned between himself and Freya.

"It is ye who must leave immediately, else I have ye thrown out by force." Her uncle motioned behind him where several horsemen, including her cousin, Ignall, rode toward the house.

Tasgall slid a look laced with pure hatred to Freya. "I am Freya's betrothed. I am in my full rights to be here."

"I am William Craig, her father's brother, and these are now my lands."

Freya rushed down and went to her uncle's side relief pouring over her.

"This changes nothing. In three days Freya and I will marry." Tasgall stalked to his horse and mounted. He glared directly at Freya. "Three days."

They watched as Tasgall, and the other man rode away.

"I dinnae think he will give up easily," her uncle said. "We have much to discuss."

"Ye came," Freya fell against him.

A SHORT TIME later her aunt, Rose, and her cousin, Sorcha arrived by carriage. Freya was delighted to see them.

THEY ALL WENT to the front room, the entire time her aunt and cousins peppering her with questions.

"Allow the lass to speak," here uncle said motioning for everyone to sit.

At the silence, Freya took a fortifying breath and described the time at sea and Beathan's death. She repeated what Beathan had overheard and how they'd managed to survive a storm at sea and arrive on the Isle of Skye. She told them how she'd sought refuge with Clan Ross and about being found by Tasgall and brought back.

"If only ye and Beathan would have come to us," her aunt said sobbing. "My poor Beathan."

Her uncle stood next to the hearth, facing the fire. Every so often he lifted his hand and wiped away tears. Heartbreak and sorrow hung in the air like a dark rain cloud.

Sorcha held Freya, her thin arms around her shoulders. By how hard her cousin cried, it seemed Sorcha was the one needed more comfort. Freya understood. The grief was brand new for them and her heart broke all over again.

Ignall was silent, as tears rolled down his cheeks. His eyes glued to the fire in the hearth. Ignall and Beathan had been close, often visiting one another.

She'd had time to grow used to the fact her handsome brother was forever gone.

She'd grieved alone the deaths of her parents and brother.

Taking a long breath, she looked at her uncle's back. "We cannae allow the home and lands that father sacrificed so much for to end in the hands of his killer."

"I should have returned to see about things sooner," her uncle said, sadness thick in his voice. "Beathan would still live. But I assumed he had things in hand, and we could wait. Then a messenger came to tell us ye'd been so grieved that ye had both gone away."

He stopped to clear his throat. "When I sent someone here to ask questions, the messenger returned with little news. Tasgall assured him ye were about to return and he would send invitations to the wedding."

"I have been praying continuously," her aunt added taking her hand.

"There is nothing to be done to change the past," Freya said gently. "And now that ye are here, ye can help me keep my father's holdings from the man responsible for his death."

"What of yer betrothal agreement?" Sorcha asked, her

pretty face pink from crying. "Can it be broken?"

"How can it nae?" her aunt cried out. "That creature is responsible for three deaths."

Her uncle frowned, his brows lowering. "It is nae that simple." He turned his attention to Freya. "How were the arrangements made?"

"His family came here, and it was announced formally before the priest. I believe that was it. His father and mine met in private to discuss the particulars. Father then informed us that upon marrying, a portion of the lands to the east would be given to us and it would be where Tasgall and I could build a home."

Her uncle nodded, stroking his bearded jaw in thought.

Freya continued. "Upon Father's death, everything would go to Beathan except for the area that was to be mine and my husband's."

"That is why he wished to kill Beathan as well," Ignall said, his face as mask of anger. "That man can nae own these lands. It can never happen."

"Under the law, a woman cannae be forced to marry against her will. As brother to yer father, this is all rightfully mine now, and I am yer guardian Freya. It would be up to me to decree what anyone marrying ye would receive."

Relief flooded through her. At the same time, she knew Tasgall. "He will nae give up easily."

Her aunt took her hand. "I must ask lass. Were ye and he ever intimate?"

The relief she'd felt was replaced with fear. Freya and Tasgall had been intimate before the betrothal.

"I-I dinnae wish to say."

Her aunt and uncle exchanged worried looks, then her uncle asked her cousins to leave the room.

Once alone, he gave her a worried look. "Freya, if ye gave yerself to him, he can claim husbandly rights and demand marriage."

"I was nae intimate with him after the betrothal."

She closed her eyes when all she could think about was Gavin and how she wished it was he who'd been her first lover.

"There is someone else now."

"Who?" both asked in unison.

"His name is Gavin Ross."

"I dinnae know if it matters," her aunt said. "If ye are nae a virgin, Tasgall can say it was he who…" She left the sentence hanging and looked to her husband. "Do ye think the clergy will insist they marry?"

"If Tasgall has thought about it and demands proof, then aye, perhaps."

"Women often give themselves to a man during moon festivals. I can say it happened then and that is was nae Tasgall. Many a lass is nae a virgin when marrying," Freya protested. "'Tis nae the times when ye were young and things were different."

Her aunt and uncle exchanged a look that said they'd not exactly been a testament to their "times".

"Let us nae worry about what has nae happened yet. For now, I will go and meet with the local laird and see what he thinks. Perhaps he has a good relationship with the local clergy."

"Thank ye. I will do anything to keep these lands out of Tasgall's hands. He has no right to demand anything." Tears trickled down her cheeks. "I am so happy to see ye. I am so glad ye are here. I have felt so alone."

"We are here now," her aunt said wiping her own tears. "I am so very sorry for all ye went through."

By the time last meal was served, Freya felt a bit more settled. Knowing that her uncle was willing to do what he could to help was comforting. She'd not brought up the subject of what they planned to do once the matter was settled. Her uncle had his own lands and home and would possibly not wish to move there.

When she prepared for bed a restlessness took over. Not knowing what would happen in the coming days made it hard to be at peace. Despite her family being there and having stayed up late into the night talking, her heart felt heavy. Each time she looked at her uncle, his resemblance to her father made her want to sob. Even his voice was so much like her father's. He seemed to understand as he caught her stealing glances at him over and again.

She pushed the shutters open and looked up at the starlit sky. Her life was forever changed. With her uncle becoming her guardian, it meant he could arrange for her to marry. Women were not meant to be alone, without protection. How long before this came to be?

Following a line of stars that formed an arrow, she wondered what Gavin did at the moment. Did he think about her? Was he fully healed now?

A part of her wished she'd confided in him earlier. Told him everything. Perhaps things would be completely different now. It was much too late for regrets.

Just the thought of him brought out warm sensations in her body. She missed seeing him, the feel of his large body when they'd hugged. His pillowy lips on hers. Freya closed her eyes and pictured his face.

The face she would in all probability never see again.

If only there was a way to get word to him. She could send a message. Let him know she was well and living with family. Inform him that she'd not wished to leave, but that she'd no other option. Yes, that is what she'd do as soon as matters with Tasgall were settled.

He'd been right to be angry and distrust her, but she was certain he would've forgiven her over time.

Unsure what to do, she left the room and went down the stairs, following the familiar route that would lead to the kitchen. Once there, she lit a small lantern and sat at the table. Placing her elbows on the surface, she cradled her chin in her hands and considered what to do. Sleep would not come, so perhaps cooking and contemplation would help.

She missed the busy work at Keep Ross. After working in the laundry all day, she'd been too tired to spend time in melancholy.

BY THE TIME the sun rose, offerings for first, second and even last meal overflowed the kitchen table. Freya took in the food, everything from fruit tarts to a pot of stew were available. Edina wouldn't have to cook at all that day.

Her aunt walked in, looking as if she'd not slept well either. She stopped in her tracks and stared at the table that was replete with food. "I thought I was dreaming when the aromas woke me several times." Moving closer, she sniffed the air. "I didnae know ye were such a good cook."

"Mother and Edina taught me," Freya replied stretching. "I'm finally getting sleepy but doubt I can sleep at all."

"Dinnae worry overly much my lass. William will take matters in hand. We talked late into the night and have more than one idea as to what can be done. All will be well."

"I want to believe ye, but nothing has gone well for me as of late," Freya replied. "I keep hoping it has all been a bad dream."

Her aunt neared and placed a hand on Freya's shoulder. "I know lass. I cannae imagine. As ye know, yer uncle is a stubborn, fearless man. He will nae allow these lands to be taken by murderers."

"Get some rest," she said pulling Freya to stand. "Go and lay down for a few moments. Whether ye sleep or not, ye need to rest."

Freya decided to draw water from the well and wash up first.

Although no one was about, as it was early yet, she felt safe knowing her uncle's men were about.

The well was just a short walk from the kitchen doors, and she hurried out to it. It was a cool morning, the breeze making it feel even more so. She'd have to heat the water before washing up as the combination of the chilly day and frigid water would not do.

Upon nearing the well, she sensed someone watching. Freya looked around but didn't see anyone. It could be Tasgall or one of his idiot friends lurked out of sight waiting for the opportunity to do harm.

She hurriedly tugged on the rope until the bucket appeared

and then she poured the water into the one she'd carried.

Once again, Freya looked around.

In the last few months, she'd become reliant on all her senses. At the moment, every instinct told her to run.

Leaving the bucket beside the well, she hitched up her skirts and raced back toward the kitchen. Her breathing caught as fear took over, making it seem as if the short distance stretched.

By the time she grabbed the door handle, she was gasping for air. The door caught, so she clutched the handle with both hands and yanked it open, throwing herself into the dimness of the house.

Once inside, she rushed into the kitchen and hurried to the window to peer outside. There was no one about.

"What are ye doing?" Her aunt came to stand next to her. "Ye look pale as a ghost."

"I thought I saw someone lurking about." Her words came out in a breathless rush. "I am nae sure. It could just be nerves."

"We have guards. If someone was about I am sure they would have seen them. Go and rest." Her aunt gave her a worried look.

THE FOLLOWING DAY, Freya insisted Ignall walk with her when she ventured outside. Once again the sensation of someone watching made her constantly look around. Ignall wasn't as inclined, hands clasped behind his back, he seemed at ease.

"Why do ye wish to be outside if ye are nae enjoying it?" he asked studying her.

"I think someone is watching. Look about," Freya whispered scanning the surroundings.

Her father had chosen the location to build the house wisely. It was on land that was slightly higher than the surroundings, keeping it safer from flooding and making it easier to see anyone approaching.

At the same time, it also meant people could watch from a distance without being seen.

Ignall pointed to a tree line. "If someone hides in the trees there is little we can do." He frowned eyes narrowed. "I do see movement."

Freya whirled to look, leaning forward and squinting in the direction Ignall motioned. Her breath caught.

Tasgall and a group of men rode toward the house.

"Hurry, we must go inside and alert yer father. He brings the village priest and constable."

Ignall shook his head. "Father has gone to meet with the Macdonald. He is nae here. He left right after first meal."

"Oh, no." Freya's breathing hitched. "What can we do?"

"Father took the stableman with him. I will speak with Tasgall and insist they wait for Father before anything can be done. They cannae force ye to marry him."

Ignall meant well, but he didn't know Tasgall.

They hurried inside not waiting for Tasgall and his men to approach and catch them outside.

CHAPTER SEVENTEEN

AFTER A NIGHT sleeping in the forest, Gavin woke in a foul mood. They'd been unable to get a room at the local tavern upon arriving late the night before. Then to his consternation, two of the men had gotten ill after eating whatever foul food they'd been served at said tavern.

They'd spent the night retching until finally falling asleep late the night before. Now he and the men woke either feeling weak from being sick, or tired from lack of rest.

The Isle of Eigg was certainly not welcoming so far.

To make matters worse, he'd decided to go to the house where he'd been told Freya lived. He'd rode close and leaving his horse behind walked closer to get a look.

Freya walked with a man, and they seemed at ease in each other's company. Not at all what he'd expected as she'd run away from a betrothal. At least that's what she'd said. She and the man didn't walk particularly close to one another, but close enough to give the impression of a good relationship between them.

He was about to leave when the man motioned toward the opposite side of the forest from where he and his men had slept. Freya and the man seemed alarmed and rushed into the house as a group of riders appeared.

Whatever happened, it wasn't good. The newcomer traveled with a group of men, including one who looked to be a priest. Interesting.

It was none of his concern, Gavin told himself riding back to the forest. At the same time, alarm bells rang in his head. Something was amiss.

He'd traveled this far to see about Freya, perhaps it was best to gather the men and pay the Craig house a visit.

No one was outside when Gavin and his men rode into the courtyard. It was a few moments before a young lad rushed to them. He seemed perplexed at their appearance.

Gavin looked to his men. "Stay here with the horses." Then he motioned to Hendry and one other. "Come with me."

They went to the front door and knocked, but no one answered. Voices carried, it was a man shouting.

Pushing the door open, he walked inside slowly, Hendry and the other man on his heels. They moved trying to be silent while following the sound of the voices.

Gavin stopped at the doorway and peered in.

"Ye cannae force Freya into marriage without her guardian present," the man who'd been walking outside with Freya shouted. "It is unlawful to force a woman into marriage."

The man who'd recently arrived made a slashing motion with his hand. "She and I are lawfully betrothed. The lass is nae a virgin. The healer will certify this."

Freya had her back to him, so Gavin could not see her expression. She stood next to a woman who had her arm around her. She remained silent, allowing the man to speak on her behalf.

"Tell them Freya." The man who'd recently arrived motioned to her aggressively. "Admit that ye and I are fully betrothed."

"I am nae yers!" Freya screamed. "Aye, I am nae a virgin, but that is nae yer doing. My lover is a Ross. He lives on Skye."

Gavin's mouth fell open, and he exchanged looks with Hendry, who gave him a wicked wink. Gavin returned what he hoped was a droll look.

"Dinnae lie. Ye cannae prove it," the angry man retorted with a humorless bark of laughter. He turned to a pair of older men, one the priest another he assumed was the healer. "Surely, ye realize she lies. As I said, after the betrothal, she and I consummated the union. If she whored herself out after that, which I doubt, then it changes nothing."

The priest didn't seem affected by the subject matter. "Miss Craig. It is yer duty to marry Tasgall. Be thankful that he is willing to overlook yer lack of morality."

"My uncle will return at any moment. Why can we nae wait for him?" Freya snapped. "Why the hurry?"

"Because I have waited long enough," the angry man, Tasgall, spat out. "Healer take her and confirm what I say is true."

The angry man grabbed Freya's wrist.

Gavin was about to step forward to stop it when the younger man, who'd she'd been walking with, rushed forward. "Take yer hands off her, now."

"Ye have no rights over me," Freya screamed yanking her arm away, but the man's hold was firm.

Tasgall moved closer to Freya, his face almost nose-to-nose with hers. "I am the only man ye have laid with. I have every right,"

"Ye dinnae," Gavin said and walked into the room. "I am her betrothed. It is I who took her virginity."

"Gavin." Freya's eyes rounded and at his pointed look, the healer released her.

There was a momentary silence as everyone in the room looked to one another and then to Gavin and the two warriors who stood behind him.

"Who the hell are ye?" the angry man demanded.

"Gavin Ross, brother to Laird Ross of Skye. I came to fetch Freya."

The man's face contorted with rage, but he seemed to have lost the ability to speak.

"She never told us about ye," the man who'd walked with Freya earlier stated looking between him and Freya. "Is this true?"

"I must speak to ye in private." Freya's voice was just above a whisper as she met Gavin's gaze.

"He lies, this changes nothing. Another one of her tricks to keep me from taking what's rightfully mine," the angry man shouted.

"Stop this," an older woman said in a firm tone. "Allow us time. Let us wait for my husband. He will clear up this matter. Let us sit and calm down. There is nae need for shouting. It is only making the situation worse."

The priest held up both hands, palms up. "I agree. We should wait. The situation has become quite confusing."

Freya's gaze took Gavin in, her eyes full of questions and what seemed like relief. He wanted nothing more than to go to her but sensed it would cause chaos to return. Instead he remained standing near the door.

"I MUST SPEAK to Freya in private," Gavin said to no one in particular as he had no idea who anyone was.

"No," the angry man stated, straightening to his full height, albeit a head shorter than Gavin. He stood with feet firmly planted and chest out. "Whoever ye really are, this has nothing to do with ye."

"I am Ignall, Freya's cousin," the man who'd been outside with Freya said. "This is my mother, her aunt. My father has gone to speak to the Macdonald about this situation." He pointed to the angry man. "That is Tasgall, an idiot."

Tasgall glared at Ignall. Gavin immediately liked Freya's cousin.

"As I said earlier, I am Gavin Ross. After my men rescued Freya and her brother from the sea, she lived there until she was taken and brought back here."

"If ye are her true betrothed, then why was she headed away from ye when I found her."

Ignoring Tasgall, Freya's aunt shooed the guards who'd come with Tasgall out of the room. They'd left reluctantly after Tasgall finally nodded.

She then spoke to another woman who he assumed was a maid. "Bring ale and oatcakes."

NO ONE SAT, everyone seeming to size up each other waiting to see who would antagonize who first. Gavin slid a glance to Freya, who seemed on the brink of tears. Her expression not giving away her thoughts. The lass was probably overwhelmed.

Her cousin, Ignall, glared with open dislike at the man called Tasgall, who maintained an air of superiority, as if considering himself to be in command of the room.

In a way Gavin supposed he was. The man was who'd brought demands and discord.

Freya's gaze met his and for a split second it was as if they were the only ones in the room. "Ye are here."

"Aye. We will talk."

"Certainly not," Tasgall said, his jaw clenched.

"Ye have nothing to say about what I do or dinnae do," Freya retorted. "Ye are a vile murderer and should be hung by yer neck."

At the words, Tasgall seemed taken aback, but he quickly regained his composure. "I had nothing to do with yer parents' death."

"Beathan overheard ye." Freya pointed at him. "He heard every word. Ye were nae careful when talking to the same two ye brought with ye today." She pointed toward the doorway. "Ye were planning to kill my brother as well. Ye didnae expect us to know."

"Stop spouting lies," Tasgall snapped taking a step forward.

Gavin had had enough. When he stepped in front of Tasgall, he was joined by Freya's cousin.

"Yer demands will nae be met. Ye should realize it by now," Ignall said.

Footsteps sounded and the men who'd come with Tasgall reentered. They stood by the door, the intent of what they'd do if Tasgall signaled evident. Hendry and the other Ross warrior sized them up and moved closer. It was evident the men from Eigg were not warriors as they visibly shrunk back.

"Go over to where yer aunt is," Gavin said to Freya in a low tone. She nodded and joined the woman, and her cousin, who were standing by the hearth.

The man Tasgall sneered at Ignall, ignoring Gavin. "Who is going to force me to leave? I have the priest and constable on my side."

Both men looked to each other, their expressions more of frustration than of standing at the ready to do Tasgall's bidding.

Tasgall motioned to Gavin and looked to his men. "Remove him from my presence."

Gavin pulled the broadsword and held it to his side.

The men didn't move, especially when Hendry growled.

The priest moved to hide behind the constable, who looked about to falter.

"This marriage will take place. I tire of this game of trying to keep me from what is lawfully my right." Tasgall gave a dry laugh. "This is all ridiculous, we all know ye are not her betrothed. My family and hers made a formal agreement. There is nothing anyone can do really to stop it." He paced back and forth seeming to not notice his men had yet to move."

When he reached the hearth, Gavin took a step forward. Tasgall met his gaze. "Why are ye really here?"

Gavin didn't reply, instead he stared at the man who's lip curved into a sneer.

"There is nae an agreement of any sort between ye and Freya. Ye should know, she is nae who ye think she is. Whatever she's said to ye is a lie. The only reason I am insisting on the marriage is because I am a man of honor. I gave my word to her father. Rest his soul."

He should have seen it coming, but Gavin had been listening to what the man spouted, not considering what he did. It was a diversion, because an instant later, Tasgall had his hand wrapped in Freya's hair and had yanked her in front of him.

A sharp dagger was pressed against Freya's throat, the blade dangerously close to breaking the skin.

Tasgall's guards froze, obviously their loyalty to him was not strong as they immediately rushed from the room.

"Priest!" Tasgall called out. "Marry us now."

The priest looked bewildered. "It is obvious that ye are deranged. I will nae in good conscious…"

"Do it or she dies," Tasgall interrupted.

When Gavin took a step closer, Tasgall pushed the tip of his dagger into Freya's throat.

Freya met Gavin's look and he saw calmness. She was trying to silently communicate with him.

"What if everyone agrees to the marriage," Gavin asked.

Everyone exchanged confused looks and he sensed Ignall was about to say something, but he held a hand up.

"Please dinnae harm the lass. She could be with child. My child."

At the words, Tasgall expression changed, his mouth fell open, but no words came out. Then he quickly recovered. "Ye are lying."

"Am I?" Gavin gave him a pointed look. "That is the reason why I am here. She told me to be with child. We argued, she left to make a point. When I came for her she was gone."

"Liar!" Tasgall screamed. He held the dagger out in Gavin's direction. "Admit it."

Freya took advantage of his distraction and thrust her small dagger into Tasgall's side. He gasped and looked down.

When he reached to yank it from his side, Freya dashed to

Gavin, and he guided her to stand behind him. She trembled against him, and never had he felt so completely full of purpose.

Tasgall threw the small dagger to the floor and held both hands to the wound. The priest and constable rushed to the injured man.

"Ye should sit," the priest said.

Tasgall refused, glaring at Freya.

CHAPTER EIGHTEEN

IN A DAZE, Freya watched as her uncle arrived and there was a flurry of conversations and activity. The entire time she remained tucked beside Gavin, his presence filling her with confidence that all would be well.

Tasgall had continued to demand the marriage take place and that he was due the lands and home as her husband.

Her uncle was like the calm in the storm.

"The terms of a marriage to Freya will change," her uncle stated looking from Tasgall to her and finally to Gavin. "Ye may live here in the house. However the property and lands now are all Ignall's."

Tasgall, who continued to hold his injured side huffed. "Ye cannae do that."

"I can," her uncle looked around the room. "This is all rightly mine. I donnae have to abide by my dead brother's agreements."

The constable cleared his throat. "That is true."

"What say ye?" Tasgall asked the priest.

"I am nae authority over agreements," the tired looking clergy replied.

There was a long silence.

"If ye demand it happen, and ye marry Freya, I will ensure ye will never own anything on these lands," her uncle stated.

Tasgall stood, bending slightly at the waist. He gave a shaky step, so the men who'd come with him had to help him out.

"I doubt this will be the last we see of him," Ignall stated what Gavin thought.

"That can be taken care of," the constable stated. "I will speak to the laird and demand Tasgall be sent away."

Gavin met her uncle's gaze, both understanding that there were other ways to keep Tasgall away. The man would die if he ever came near Freya again.

HER AUNT CAME and took Freya's hand. "Come ye need to wash up."

Seeming too overwhelmed to argue, she allowed herself to be lead from the room.

WHY HAD HE come?

The last time they'd spoken, he'd not been inclined to help her anymore, but had agreed with the laird that she go to Uist to work at his cousin's keep. She'd thought never to see him again and yet he'd arrived there at her home, with considered perfect timing and professed to not only being her betrothed, but the father of a child they'd conceived.

Nothing made sense.

Freya stood in the center of her bedchamber and peered down at her trembling hands, noticing for the first time the blood on her right hand. Dark droplets on her hand, forearm, and the front of her blouse. She scratched at it wanting it gone.

"Freya." Her aunt pushed a goblet into her hand. "Drink it. Ye are shaking."

She lifted the cup to her lips and sipped the honeyed mead. "I dinnae know what to do."

"For now we wait. Then ye will have a hot bath and rest. Yer uncle will speak with the priest and constable," her aunt said in a soft soothing voice.

Perhaps it was the honeyed mead, or the soothing tone in her aunt's voice, but suddenly she felt very tired. Freya nodded and went to sit on the bed to await the bath to be brought.

FREYA'S EYES FLEW open. Through the open window, she could see it was late in the day. Next to her bed, Gavin sat in a chair, his eyes trained on her.

For a moment neither said anything.

"Why did ye come?" Freya asked. "Why are ye here?"

His Adam's apple bobbed. "For ye. When I found out that ye had been taken by force, I had to ensure ye were nae harmed."

"Ye are nae responsible for me." Freya fiddled with the blankets, more to keep her hands busy as she wasn't sure what to do.

Gavin let out a long sigh. "Ye left because of what I said. I should have listened to ye. I was prideful and refused to listen to ye. Instead of ensuring yer well-being, I told ye to go."

"I was a burden to yer clan. I could have explained more. I do nae blame ye for thinking I could bring danger. Perhaps I did," she said.

After a moment, he met her eyes. "Why did ye nae tell me everything? I would have protected ye."

"How was I to know ye would nae send me back here? Yer clan is large. I was afraid ye were friendly with Tasgall's family."

His gaze fell. "I suppose there's naught to be done about it now."

There was something more she wished to know, but the questions became lodged in her throat. Finally she fortified herself.

"How do ye feel. Ye should nae be traveling so far after yer injury."

Gavin shrugged. "I am well enough to be here and ensure ye are."

"Why did ye say we were betrothed and that I could be with child?"

The corners of his lips twitched. "Both are a possibility."

"We are nae betrothed, and I am nae with child." Freya crossed her arms. "I do, however, thank ye for standing up for me."

Gavin nodded.

"When will ye go back to Skye?" Freya didn't want to know the answer. What she wished was to ask him to stay. There was nothing more she wished for than to spend time with him. Just his presence alone made her feel safe and protected.

"Do ye wish me to go?"

The question was not a complicated one, but in so many ways so very hard to answer. Freya decided to be honest.

"I dinnae." She looked at him. "I wish for more time with ye."

He reached for her hand, taking it in his much larger one. "I-I… err…" He stumbled over the words. Was he about to divulge something horrifying?

"I came because I am in love with ye, and I found that I cannae survive without ye in my life." He closed his eyes as if in pain, then opened them, the deep green had darkened as they met hers. "That day in the forest. It cannae be the only time."

Her cheeks warmed at the reference and immediately their intimate moment flashed in her mind. The gasps. The joining of their bodies. The way they'd kissed with a combination of desperation and desire. It had been perfect and passionate. Two souls finding each other after a lifetime of searching.

Her heart began to pound. "Thinking that I'd never see ye again has been physically painful. I thought it was this place, that I didn't feel at home because everything had changed. My family. Me. But now that ye are here, it is as if the heartbeat has returned. The house has come back to life. Ye brought my heart with ye."

Gavin's lips parted in surprise and then curved before he asked, "Can I kiss ye?"

All Freya could do was nod and instantly his lips were over hers. It was as if she'd been holding her breath since the day she'd left Ross keep because every ounce of her being came to life. A lightness engulfed her as she clung to him. Her arms surrounded his neck, bringing him closer.

"Gavin," she whispered into his ear when they broke the kiss. "Ye came for me."

"I did." He pressed kisses to the side of her face, trailing his lips down her throat. "I could nae breathe."

He pulled back but continued to hold her. If she were to die in that instant Freya would not mind. Being in his arms was as close to heaven as she could get while still on earth.

After everything she'd been through was he to be her reward? Was life making up for all that had been taken from her?

Tears flowed freely down her face. "Promise never to leave me. Tell me ye will always be with me."

"I promise to remain by yer side always," Gavin whispered. "Unless I go to battle, or have to visit my brother, or do my duties as guard."

She pulled back to look at the sly grin on his face. He teased her.

Freya laughed.

It had been so very long since she'd laughed.

LAST MEAL WAS a somber event, everyone seeming to be in his or her own thoughts. Freya slid glances to Gavin who spoke with her uncle. They discussed the differences between Skye and Eigg. Every so often Ignall would join in adding information about where they worked.

Freya leaned to her aunt. "Uncle speaks as if he plans to return home. What about this house and lands? What will happen, will Ignall remain?"

Her aunt smiled and patted her hand. "William and I will return home Freya. Ignall will remain here." She slid a look to Gavin. "He is quite bonnie. Do ye plan to live here or on Skye?"

At Freya's confusion, Sorcha spoke up. "He did say ye are betrothed. Ye will have to decide where to live."

"Let us give it a pair of days. We've had enough excitement for one day," her aunt stated.

Gavin looked toward their end of the table as if trying to decipher what they spoke about. Freya couldn't help the flush of heat to her cheeks when their eyes met.

"We may have to plan a wedding soon as possible, lest there truly be a bairn," her aunt said with a soft chuckle.

"Mother!" Sorcha exclaimed a wide grin spreading across her pretty face.

When the meal ended, Gavin took Freya's elbow. "Would ye like to walk?"

"I do need air," Freya agreed much too quickly. Questions were swimming in her head since they'd kissed. There were decisions to be made and regardless of Gavin's proclamations of love for her, there was the issue of him being a laird's brother. He could not marry without his brother's permission. She knew Gavin enough to know that his first loyalty was to the clan.

The air was cool, but Freya barely felt it. Walking beside Gavin, her skin immediately heated. They walked to a garden area, and he looked around. "I can see why ye love it here. The lands are beautiful."

She followed his line of sight to the horizon where the sun was setting and then across to where a stream meandered around a grouping of trees and on into the forest. It was indeed a lovely view.

"What happens now?" Freya asked while attempting to keep her breathing even. "I imagine ye will have to speak to yer brother."

Gavin nodded. "Aye. I must return to Skye. There are matters that have to be dealt with."

There was something akin to trepidation in his expression,

as if he expected she would rebuff him.

"Freya," he began and took her hands. "I have nae asked. Are ye willing to marry me then?"

She couldn't keep from smiling up at him. "I wish for nothing more than to be yer wife."

"I sense there is a condition," Gavin stated.

"My aunt and uncle wish to know if we marry where will we live. They wish to return to their own land and not live here. A decision will have to be made about this house and land, if we go to Skye, Ignall will have to come here to live. Or perhaps the lands will be sold. I donnae know. It is ironic since I've fought so hard to keep them and now…" She wasn't sure how to finish the statement.

Gavin's brow furrowed. "My clan needs me Freya. There is the matter of the men attacking and…" He stopped and looked around, his eyes moving past her. "I dinnae wish to take ye away from yer home."

Blinking back tears, she nodded. "I understand. Of course I do. I do ask that we marry here. After, then we can go."

She was thankful when he pulled her against him, his strong arms like a harbor. Freya lifted her face, offering him her mouth. Gavin pressed his lips to hers, kissing a trail across her mouth before prodding at the crease with his tongue.

When his tongue delved into her mouth, Freya's knees weakened, the intrusion a reminder of their more intimate time together.

A moan escaped when he lifted her guiding her to wrap her legs around his waist. He turned to the wall of the house, her back pressing against the solid stone as he continued to kiss her, his hands sliding down her sides to cup her breasts and pushing them to free them from the confines of her blouse.

Everything disappeared except for Gavin. Birdsong was overtaken by the sounds of their kisses and gasps of breaths. The hardness of his body crushing hers was like a balm to her soul. Once again a lightness filled her competing with the heat of passion that pooled between her legs.

When his mouth closed over the tip of her breast, Freya had to bite her bottom lip to keep quiet. Each time he sucked harder, throbs of desire shot to her center, filling her with so much need, she began to rub her core against him.

"Oh," Freya hissed. "Ye must stop. I cannae take more."

Suddenly, he lowered her to the ground, shoving her skirts down. Freya swayed and was about to ask why he stopped when a man appeared. It was the guard Hendry.

"Her aunt walked out to find ye," he said looking at Freya. "I volunteered to complete the task." He gave Gavin a knowing look.

Freya's hands flew up to her blouse thankfully, the top had fallen down and covered her breasts.

"Thank ye. I will go inside momentarily," she replied in a breathy voice.

Whether the man heard or not, she couldn't tell as he was already rounding the building back the way he'd come.

"We best go inside," Freya said pushing past Gavin and then stopping short. "We didnae decide anything."

He guided her toward the front of the house. "Will ye return with me to Skye?" He gave her the choice and for that she'd follow him anywhere.

CHAPTER NINETEEN

One Month Later
Isle of Eigg

THE WEDDING CEREMONY was simple by the standards of someone of her wealth, but Freya wouldn't have had it any other way.

Her aunt fussed over every detail as Lady Ross, her cousin Sorcha, and Gavin's brothers' wives helped out with what they could.

It was wonderful to be surrounded by women who cared for her.

Wearing a flowing gown that had been her mother's Freya felt beautiful that day. Her aunt pinned her hair in place and took a step back. "Perfect."

Just then movement from the far corner of the room made Freya look, for a whisper of a moment, her mother stood there and then the image faded. It was so fast that she wasn't sure she had seen it. At her startled expression, everyone looked to the corner.

"What is it?" her aunt asked in a soft voice.

"I thought to have seen Mother." Freya shook her head. "I'm sure it is just that I am nervous."

Her aunt took her hand. "Of course it was her. Yer mother would nae miss this moment."

Freya blinked away happy tears. "She would nae."

GAVIN STOOD PROUDLY at the front of the chapel. He wore the Ross clan colors of green and black draped over his shoulder, his kilt was solid black, and a tunic made of white fine linen. Next to him stood his brothers, each striking in their own right.

On her uncle's arm, she walked down the center of the room, not seeing anyone but her handsome husband to be, his gaze never wavering from hers.

She took a deep breath imagining that if things were different, her brother and father would have been involved in the marriage ceremony as well.

Just then Gavin's other two brothers moved away, leaving only Gavin and Munro. Freya gathered that of his three brothers, Gavin was closest to him.

As she made her way to the front of the room, it was strange that there were very few people in attendance other than the family, some of the servants, and Laird Macdonald.

In a way Freya preferred it. She wished to celebrate, but her heart was also broken that her parents and brother were not there.

The exchange of vows seemed to go swiftly, each repeating after the young vicar from a neighboring village whom she'd picked to do the wedding, not wishing for the priest who'd presided over her betrothal to Tasgall to be who married her to Gavin.

Before she realized it, Gavin's lips were on hers as they sealed their commitment to one another, and she wondered exactly how it was possible to have missed whatever it was the vicar had said.

Gavin gave her a quizzical look as their families headed toward them. "Is something wrong?"

"No… not exactly. 'Tis just that I wanted to commit every moment to memory, and I seem to have missed parts of it. It went much too fast."

His lips curved. "It did."

They were ushered into the house to the large room where her parents had often entertained. There was just enough room for everyone, making Freya glad they'd not invited too many people.

Someone, probably her aunt, had hired musicians, and the music filled the room. When she saw the display of food set out by Edina, Freya had to blink back tears. It was the kind of display her mother would have chosen.

She turned searching for the older woman and found her standing with her hands clasped in front watching from the doorway.

Their eyes met; Edina's eyes watery as she held back tears. How many times had her mother and Edina discussed details for her wedding?

Freya lifted to her toes and placed a kiss to Gavin's jaw. "I will return in a moment."

She made a beeline for Edina, throwing herself into the older woman's arms and both began to cry.

Before long they were surrounded by her aunt and Gavin's mother, each asking what happened.

Edina cleared her throat, wiping her eyes with the sleeve of her blouse. "We remember how much Freya's mother had looked forward to this day."

"This is nae a day for tears, but for celebration," her aunt proclaimed. "Yer mother would have nae wished for sorrow, but for happiness on this day."

Freya nodded. "I am so very happy." She looked across the room noting Gavin watching them. "He will ensure it."

"Aye, my son would rather die than cause ye a sadness." Lady Ross took her hand. "Come let us celebrate."

The musicians were instructed to play lively music as Freya and Gavin, and their guests, celebrated. The food was delicious and only the best ales were served. After the meal, there was dancing until late into the night.

"Wife," Gavin whispered into her ear. "It is time for us to bid everyone a good night."

CHAPTER TWENTY

Clothing was dispensed with haste, articles falling askew across the bedchamber's floor, some landing across chairs.

Too impatient to wait, Gavin had practically torn the layers of clothing from her body until he left his bride totally naked. Her beautiful body enhanced by the flames in the hearth.

For a moment they hesitated next to the bed, unsure who would move first.

Freya was hungry for his body, her eyes taking in the expanse of his chest before traveling down past his stomach and hesitating at his already engorged sex. Her intake of breath was like a caress across his heated core.

Unable to withstand it, he lifted the beauty and placed her on the bedding. It was impossible not to gawk at the vision. From her full breasts to the delicate indentation of her waist to the flare of her soft hips she more than he could have ever dreamed for.

Away from her would be the makings of sleepless nights, tossing and turning wishing to be able to reach out and slide a hand from the silken waves down the soft skin.

The way Gavin openly studied her body made Freya reach for

the edge of a blanket, but he stopped her. Taking her hand, he held it. "I can never tire of looking at ye like this. A beautiful sight to behold."

After holding her gaze, his eyes down to her breasts and then swept to between her legs, which gave her the opportunity to study him in turn. She could repeat his words when describing him.

The man was perfectly made as if sculped masterfully from a stone. Muscular arms and thighs, slender hips and ridged stomach.

Finally, he came over her, the weight of his body making her sink into the bedding. It felt wonderful when his mouth finally covered hers. The kiss explored and took from her what she offered and more.

Every inch of her body was live, each touch of his hands sending tingles of excitement throughout.

A moan escaped when his tongue traced circles around the tip of her right breast before moving across to pay the other homage. Freya moaned loudly, allowing herself freedom to not hold back one single bit. This was her night to enjoy, and she would fully.

They'd not been intimate, deciding to wait until the wedding night and it had been excruciating.

"I want ye so badly," Freya whispered into his ear then licking along the edge of it. She was rewarded by his intake of breath and soft grunt.

She slid her right foot up the side of his leg, loving the feel of the firm muscular tones.

"I cannae wait," Gavin said coming over her. "If it happens too quickly, I promise to make it longer for ye next time."

In truth she was as desperate for him. When he took himself in hand, Freya almost screamed for him to hurry. Finally, he prodded at her entrance, and she practically jumped out of her skin.

"Impatient are ye?" Gavin attempted to tease, but his breathlessness gave away that he too wanted to hurry.

"Gaaaviiin," she moaned moving her hips up in an attempt to take him.

When he slid between her sex, the length rubbing against the most intimate part, it was as if a bolt of lightning struck, Freya's back arched as she let out a loud gasp.

Gavin's lips curved and he slid his hardness up and down the same spot until she cried out.

"Ye are as much in need as I am," he whispered into her ear as he slowly inched into her body.

Freya was incoherent, still floating from the surprising reaction of her body to his.

When he thrust fully into her, Freya moaned.

He filled her completely, the silky staff sliding easily in and out of her slick moistness. Freya grasped his bottom with both hands loving the feel of his body, the way the muscles contracted with each movement.

In that moment they were one, fully joined in a way that only a man and a woman could be. Gavin was hers. Her husband, her lover.

They were and always would be, husband and wife.

Gavin pulled out, not all the way, then sunk back into her. Freya gripped his shoulders and lifted her legs and wrapped them around his waist to allow him more freedom of movement.

He continued plunging in and pulling out. Each time Freya urged him to move faster, to not stop, her heated sex demanding to be drenched, while at the same time growing hotter.

Hard as she fought to stay grounded, it was impossible. An all-consuming pull pushed into the edges of her consciousness until she had no choice but to let go and fall into a heavenly abyss.

In a haze she realized Gavin continued moving, his body's own need taking over, all sense or rhythm dissolved. The sounds of their bodies colliding, and his deep moans filled the air around her ears, it was a delightfully sensual sound.

He tensed, then let out a guttural moan, his body trembling.

Freya wrapped her arms and tightened legs around him wanting to soak up every bit of what he gave.

When he collapsed atop her they remained joined.

"I love ye Gavin," Freya whispered, her breathing ragged. "So very much."

He lifted to look at her. "I am glad because I love ye as well."

Rolling from her, he brought her against his side, his arms around her, cradling Freya as if she were the most precious of things.

They were silent for a moment, then his breathing became slow and steady. Freya looked up to see that he'd fallen asleep.

A HAND SLIDING down from her side to her hip woke Freya. She wasn't sure how long to have slept, but the fire in the hearth was only embers now.

Her breathing hitched when Gavin slid his hand from her

hip and his fingers moved to between her legs. She bit down on her lip, but the whimper escaped nonetheless when he circled the nub between her folds, his breaths fanning across the side of her face.

Gavin brought her to the edge rolling her to her side facing away from him. "I need ye again," he murmured into her ear, his thickness pushing into her already burning sex.

With each movement in and out of her, his fingers continued their wonderful assault. Freya cried out and crested her sex tightening around his.

Hands on her hips, Gavin drove in and out of her in a steady rhythm until she began meeting his thrusts, pushing backward.

His fingers dug into her flesh as he buried deeper into her and spilled.

Freya fell into a sated sleep.

THEY WERE AWAKENED by soft knocks, then Edina and another young woman brough in trays with food and beverages, which they left on a table by the hearth. Neither looked to the bed nor spoke.

Other than that, no one came to the bedchamber. Gavin guessed it was their family's attempt to give them time alone to discuss the particulars of their upcoming days.

It was hard to keep his mind focused as Freya rose from the bed, her mussed hair a tangled mess fell past her shoulders and over the tops of her small but shapely breasts. Her slender body beckoned, and he had a hard time keeping from pulling her back to the bed. Thankfully, or perhaps not, she donned a robe and tied a belt around her waist. As much as he hated that she covered herself, it helped him to think clearer.

He rose from the bed and wrapped the discarded tartan around his hips and then joined her at the small table.

"I have a wedding gift for ye," he said as he settled into the chair.

Freya's gaze moved from him to scan the room. "What is it?"

Taking her hand, he brought it to his lips. "I am going to live here with ye. It has been decided."

For a moment he thought she was disappointed as her face crumpled and Freya covered it with both hands. But then she leaped from her chair and threw herself into his lap covering his face with kisses. He'd never been so sure of a decision in his life.

"I cannae believe it. Say it again Gavin, so I know it is true."

"Alexander agrees. Although there is much to be done in Skye, he thinks it would be best for me to live here in this beautiful home and land with ye."

She kissed him on the lips, then on each cheek. "I am nae sure what to say. I am so very happy. What of the attackers? What of yer duties with the clan?"

"Knox, Munro and Cynden will help Alex. I can go and help if they need me," he told her. It had been his eldest brother who'd suggested that Gavin remain there. On Skye he would not have his own region, his own home since he was third born. Here he would have more than on Skye and it would add to Clan Ross holdings. It was a win for both his and

Freya's family.

"I spoke to yer uncle, and he is relieved that his brother's lands will be well taken care of and that ye will continue to live here. Ignall is yer uncle's only male heir and expects to take over that land once it is time."

Freya's mouth covered his, her inexperienced kiss the sweetest he'd ever tasted.

Her eyes were shiny with unshed tears when meeting his. "Ye have made me so happy. I am nae sure to ever be able to demonstrate to ye how glad I am to be yer wife." Freya wiped an errant tear. "Thank ye." She kissed him again.

"Thank ye." She pressed her lips to Gavin's jaw. "So much for the perfect gift."

Gently, he pushed her from his lap and stood. When he lifted her into his arms and walked toward the bed, Freya gasped.

"Again?"

"Aye... Again."

They remained in the bedchamber for the rest of the day.

EPILOGUE

Two days later

ALEXANDER ROSS STOOD on the deck of one of the birlinns and watched the waves lapping gently against the side. The wind blew his raven black hair across his face, as he absently pushed it back.

Life was progressing much too quickly for his liking. Once back on Skye, there would be much to deal with. And though he was happy for his brother, what he told Gavin was true. If another battle came to be, his hawk-like vision would be sorely missed.

All of his brothers were now married and of his three brothers only Cynden remained at home. Both Munro and Gavin had married and taken over their wives' lands.

A choice he wouldn't have. Alex didn't mind, his holdings were vast and with Cynden and Knox living with him, he could handle things.

As laird of the vast Ross lands on Skye, if he were ever to marry, which he doubted would be anytime soon, his wife would be moving to live with him.

Alexander closed his eyes trying to envision who he'd marry. If he were ever to do so, which was doubtful.

His marriage would not be for love, but for the benefit of the clan. Which suited him fine. The last thing he needed was to act like a besotted fool over some pretty lass. Being in love could prove dangerous for a laird.

As Laird, his primary focus would have to always be on the wellbeing of the clan's people.

At the moment, his most important task awaited.

He would hunt down whoever the band of attackers were, and they would be dealt with. Then he would begin the work of ensuring his people were ready and prepared for winter.

"Land!" someone called out as the shore of Skye came into view. Alex let out a long breath.

Home.

Will Alexander Ross fall in love? Find out in The Raven.

About the Author

Enticing. Engaging. Romance.

USA Today Bestselling Author Hildie McQueen writes strong brooding alpha Highlanders who meet their match in feisty brave heroines. If you like stories with a mixture of passion, action, drama and humor, you will love Hildie's storytelling where love wins every single time!

A fan of all things pink, travel, and stationery, Hildie resides in eastern Georgia, USA, with her super-hero husband Kurt and three little yappy dogs.

Let's stay in touch, join my NEWSLETTER for free reads, previews of upcoming releases and news about my world!

Printed in Great Britain
by Amazon